D1128880

SPECIAL MESSAGE TO READERS

This book is published under the auspices of

THE ULVERSCROFT FOUNDATION

(registered charity No. 264873 UK)

Established in 1972 to provide funds for research, diagnosis and treatment of eye diseases. Examples of contributions made are: —

A Children's Assessment Unit at
Moorfield's Hospital, London.

•

Twin operating theatres at the
Western Ophthalmic Hospital, London.

•

A Chair of Ophthalmology at the
Royal Australian College of Ophthalmologists.

•

The Ulverscroft Children's Eye Unit at the
Great Ormond Street Hospital For Sick Children,
London.

You can help further the work of the Foundation by making a donation or leaving a legacy. Every contribution, no matter how small, is received with gratitude. Please write for details to:

THE ULVERSCROFT FOUNDATION,
The Green, Bradgate Road, Anstey,
Leicester LE7 7FU, England.
Telephone: (0116) 236 4325

In Australia write to:
THE ULVERSCROFT FOUNDATION,
c/o The Royal Australian and New Zealand
College of Ophthalmologists,
94-98 Chalmers Street, Surry Hills,
N.S.W. 2010, Australia

MEET JIMMY STRANGE

Jimmy Strange was a mysterious young man who'd turn up when he was least expected; wherever there was trouble, he'd appear from behind some dark corner. No one knew much about him, though he was always a gentleman. He was never short of money, but where it came from no one knew. He wasn't a crook — yet they did say he could break into a house with the best of them — but always in a good cause . . .

ERNEST DUDLEY

MEET JIMMY STRANGE

Complete and Unabridged

LINFORD
Leicester

First published in Great Britain

First Linford Edition
published 2011

Copyright © 1948 by Ernest Dudley
Copyright © 2011 by Susan Dudley-Allen
All rights reserved

British Library CIP Data

Dudley, Ernest.
  Meet Jimmy Strange. - -
  (Linford mystery library)
  1. Strange, Jimmy (Fictitious character)- -
  Fiction. 2. Detective and mystery stories.
  3. Large type books.
  I. Title II. Series
  823.9′14–dc22

  ISBN 978–1–44480–532–1

Published by
F. A. Thorpe (Publishing)
Anstey, Leicestershire

Set by Words & Graphics Ltd.
Anstey, Leicestershire
Printed and bound in Great Britain by
T. J. International Ltd., Padstow, Cornwall

This book is printed on acid-free paper

For
MY DAUGHTER SUSAN
Without whose helpful advice and
criticism Jimmy's adventures would
have been written in roughly
half the time

1

The Girl at the Rainbow

Whistles shrilled warningly, carriage doors slammed and the Scots express gathered itself preparatory to pulling out on its long run from King's Cross to the North.

'Goodbye, Jimmy. Take care of yourself.'

'Goodbye, Gail — I suppose you must go?'

'Must, darling. Uncle would have a fit if I didn't turn up now.'

'You could wire him you'd been run over or something.'

She laughed delightfully. 'The things you think of! No, I've put him off so often. I can't disappoint him again.'

'It'll be hell without you.'

'It'll be hell without you. But I'll only be away three weeks.'

'Might as well be three centuries — it'll seem as long.'

'Darling!'

The train began to slide along the platform. Keeping pace with it, Jimmy held on to her hand. He thought she had never seemed so attractive as she did at this moment

'Oh, Gail, I suppose — er — that is — '

The train was gaining momentum. He had to walk quickly.

'What is it, Jimmy?'

'Nothing really. I was only wondering — '

'You'd better let me go, or you'll be running alongside all the way up to Scotland! What d'you want to ask me?'

'I — oh, it'll keep till you come back.'

He let go her hand, and as she drew away with ever-increasing speed, she called back, 'Oh, you are irritating! What is it?'

He waved to her.

'Tell you in three weeks' time!'

She pouted at him.

'I hope it's worth waiting for.'

He grinned but didn't answer. She waved and then was gone.

As he watched the train speeding on its

journey, Jimmy Strange told himself that had been the nearest thing yet. Another moment and he'd have asked her to marry him. He fairly shivered at the thought. What the devil would he think up next? What sort of a sentimental chump was he turning out to be? Just because she was going away for three weeks to visit an uncle in Scotland . . .

Really, he'd better pull himself together.

Of course, Gail was adorable, the most alluring girl he'd known — and his experience had not exactly been negligible in that respect. But marriage was something else. He'd worn his heart on his sleeve for too long now, and knew that was the best place to keep it for such a character as he. Better there than attached to any woman's apron strings, no matter how attractive she was.

Yes, it had been a lucky escape!

He lit a cigarette and drifted into the station bar and downed a double Scotch. No doubt about it, he felt pretty low at the prospect of not seeing Gail for three weeks. He had another drink while he pondered how he should wear out the rest of the morning. It was a bright spring day, and he suddenly decided it would be an attractive notion to pop down into the country for lunch. There was that place near Marlow, the *Rainbow Inn*. A good spot, he remembered. He'd meant to take Gail down there, but somehow never had. He strolled out into the sunshine and found his car. Presently he was nosing his way through the traffic round Hyde Park Corner and headed for the Great West Road.

An hour or so later he broke off in the middle of the tune he was whistling, and with a narrowed gaze took his foot off the accelerator. About twenty yards ahead of him, standing in the middle of the country road, stood a young man, waving his arms frantically.

Jimmy pulled up.

'Anything wrong?' he called.

'Which is the quickest way to the village? Please tell me . . . ' the other gasped urgently. He was obviously distraught, his eyes wild, his face pale and harassed.

'Keep straight on.'

'Thank you. How far? Is there somewhere I can telephone?'

'It's about a mile. You'll find an hotel
you can 'phone from . . . '

'Oh, good!' He pushed his hand
through his hair as if trying to concentrate his thoughts. 'Is the hotel called the
— the . . . ?' He paused, racking his
memory.

'It's called the 'Rainbow'.'

'That's it. The 'Rainbow'!'

Jimmy looked closely at the other. He
noted his hands clenched and unclenched
spasmodically, and that though his build
was athletic, his features suggested he had
been ill recently. He said:

'I'll drive you there. Hop in.'

'Would you? Oh, thank you so much.
I'm in a dreadful hurry.'

'We'll be there in a jiffy.'

Jimmy tugged at the self-starter. The
engine coughed and spluttered, and the
starter stuck rigidly. It had jammed.

He fiddled with it in an effort to free it.

'Damn! It's stuck!'

'You must get it to go!'

The other's voice was high-pitched

5

with anxiety. 'It's a matter of life and death. I must get there . . . '

'Have to crank her,' Jimmy grunted. He grabbed the crank-handle from under the seat and went to the front of the car. The young man watched him with ill-concealed agitation. Suddenly from round the corner came the sound of an approaching car. At once he clambered out of his seat and rushed towards Jimmy.

'A car!' he babbled. 'They're after me! They mustn't catch me!' And he set off along the road, running and stumbling in terrified haste.

Jimmy watched him with a puzzled frown, then shrugged. A dark saloon swung round the corner, shot past him and overtook his odd passenger. As it pulled up alongside, the fleeing figure gave a backward terror-stricken glance and, turning to a five-barred gate, desperately started to climb over it.

Three men jumped out of the car and chased after him. Two of the figures were heavily built, the other who followed more leisurely was a dapper figure in formal striped trousers and dark jacket.

They overtook their quarry just as he was half over the gate. They hauled him back. One of the men adroitly seized the fugitive's jacket collar and jerked it downwards, so that his arms were pinioned. Jimmy lit a cigarette as he watched the scene. Now he moved towards the group.

The captive struggled and twisted to call out as he approached:

'Don't let them take me! They'll kill me — they'll — !'

One of the big men clapped his hand over the other's mouth and silenced him.

As Jimmy strolled up casually, the man in striped trousers was blinking at the young man through heavy, horn-rimmed spectacles.

'Now, Carthew — calm yourself. We are friends,' he murmured soothingly. 'We're here to look after you.'

'I won't come back!' was the almost hysterical response. 'I won't!'

'You must not excite yourself. No one's going to hurt you.'

Jimmy said: 'What goes on?'

Striped trousers turned to him and

surveyed him for a moment. Then he shook his head gravely. He nodded towards the man behind him.

'This is a patient of mine.'

Jimmy didn't say anything. Just lazily drew at his cigarette and slowly exhaled a cloud of smoke.

'Suffers from delusions, I'm afraid,' Striped Trousers went on, adopting a confidential tone. 'You've had a narrow escape; he's dangerous. Homicidal, in fact.' He gestured to the burlier of the two large men. 'He attacked one of my male nurses just now and escaped from my nursing home.'

Jimmy said: 'You the doctor?'

The other nodded.

'Markham's my name, Dr. Markham. Great responsibility you know, these cases are.' Again he wagged his head. 'Very sad.'

Jimmy glanced at his patient, and could not help feeling somewhat sympathetic towards him. He was looking at him pleadingly. 'Don't let them take me,' he gasped brokenly. 'They'll kill me. They'll — '

Dr. Markham broke in imperatively:

8

'Come along now, Carthew, we must be getting back.'

'I won't come!'

'It's no use being obstinate,' said the doctor smoothly. 'You don't want me to have to ask Jackson to use force — '

'You're not going to take me — '

'Or would you prefer my dear boy, that I resorted to the hypodermic?'

'No, no! Don't do that!'

Carthew seemed suddenly to grow limp, all the stuffing knocked out of him by the implied threat in the other's question. He muttered: 'I'll come — only don't use the hypodermic.'

'That's a sensible fellow,' Dr. Markham said agreeably, and motioned to the two men to lead their charge away. He sighed regretfully as he turned to Jimmy again. 'He's been a great burden to his family. Very sad. Very sad. I tell you, they need some handling, these poor souls.'

'You seem to have the knack all right, anyway.'

'Just have to treat them like children.' He gave Jimmy a keen look from behind his horn-rims, then said briskly: 'Well, good morning.' And he hurried after the others.

Jimmy returned to his own car. As he bent to crank the engine, he glanced speculatively after the doctor's black saloon as it sped past him and disappeared round the corner the way it had come.

Somehow he felt vaguely dissatisfied about the little drama that had just been enacted before him. Then he shrugged. He tried to tell himself it was none of his business and he could have done nothing about it in such circumstances. He supposed that inmates of mental homes did sometimes escape, and had to be recaptured by firm persuasion. All the same, he couldn't help feeling that there was something about the affair he didn't like. He made a mental note to check the bona fides of Dr. Markham in the *Medical Directory*.

He cranked the car, and the self-starter freed itself after the engine ticked over for a minute or two. He drove towards the village. A glance at his watch told him it was now getting on for lunchtime. He was approaching the *Rainbow Inn*, about which Dr. Markham's patient had inquired.

Jimmy drew up. He decided he could lunch here, and at the same time perhaps discover the link between the inn and the strange young man.

After an excellent lunch he found himself a quiet corner on the terrace overlooking the garden. An old, round-shouldered waiter followed him out of the dining room.

'Will you take coffee, sir?'

'Thanks. Bring me a Benedictine, too, will you?'

'A Benedictine, yessir.'

'And I think I could use a cigar.'

'A cigar, yessir.'

'Double Corona, if you have one.'

'A Double Corona, yessir.'

Jimmy relaxed contentedly, his thoughts veering between the incident of the escaped mental patient and Gail, who by now was well on her way North. He sighed somewhat wistfully, and then sat up with a jerk. Unmistakably he could hear sounds of someone sobbing. A woman. The sobs grew louder, and Jimmy got to his feet and looked round for the direction whence they came. The table next to him was surrounded by a rose arbour. He pushed through the trellis archway, took one look — and instinctively straightened his tie.

He said: 'Forgive me butting in, but — er — is there anything I can do?'

The girl looked up at him with a startled expression. Jimmy noted with keen appreciation that her wide eyes were like dew-misted violets shaded by long dark lashes, and her nose was irresistibly tip-tilted.

'Did I make you jump?' he apologized gently. 'I'm sorry.'

She said: 'I didn't think anyone would hear me.'

He nodded understandingly. 'I know. Nothing like a nice cry in private, so don't let me spoil your party. Here, try my handkerchief.'

'Th — thank you.'

Jimmy sat down on a garden chair opposite her. He was just congratulating himself on the fortunate chance that had precipitated him into the company of such a remarkably attractive specimen of femininity when the waiter appeared round the archway, bearing a tray.

'Your coffee and liqueur, sir — oh, beg pardon, I didn't see — '

'That's all right, George. The lady's a little upset.'

'Upset, yessir.'

'Perhaps you'd bring a little something to calm her?'

'Calm her, yessir.'

'Such as a spot of fine old brandy.'

'Fine old bra — '

'You'd save an awful lot of time,' Jimmy interrupted him shortly, 'if you'd refrain from repeating everything I say, and popped off and did it.'

'Did it, yessir,' repeated the waiter incorrigibly, muttering as he retreated: 'Fine old brandy.'

'I give up!' sighed Jimmy.

The girl said rather unsteadily: 'It's most kind of you. But I couldn't drink anything.'

'Oh, but you don't have to drink it. You just sip it, very slowly.'

'But I — '

'Do you a world of good,' he said firmly. He looked at her searchingly. 'By the way, we haven't met before, have we?'

'I — I don't think so.'

'Funny, I seem to know your face.' He whistled suddenly. 'Why, of course!'

'What is it?'

'Only that I've a pretty good idea why you're crying.'

'How — how d'you mean?'

'It's because of your brother, isn't it?'

She gave a gasp of surprise.

'How can you possibly know my brother?' she asked quickly.

'I met him this morning.'

She stared at him. 'But — but you couldn't have done.'

'His name's Carthew.'

'Yes, it is.'

'He's in a nursing home near by and — here comes your brandy.'

'Brandy for the lady, sir.'

'Oh, you won't forget my Double Corona?' Jimmy said, adding quickly, in unison with the other:

'Double Corona, yessir!'

The waiter threw him a startled glance

and shuffled away. Jimmy chuckled after him. The girl was saying as he handed her the drink:

'What did you mean about seeing Philip — my brother — today? Dr. Markham wouldn't allow me to see him.'

'Is that so?'

'He told me Philip's much too ill.'

'Really?' He gazed at her quizzically, taking a mental inventory of other attractive features. He mused: 'The likeness is amazing.'

She nodded. 'We are very much alike.'

The waiter returned, and obviously with a supreme effort proffered a box of cigars without a word. Jimmy grinned up at him and carefully made his choice. Gravely — and silently — the waiter withdrew.

Through a cloud of aromatic cigar smoke Jimmy eyed the girl.

'So . . . Dr. Markham says your brother's very ill?'

She nodded. Her face was shadowed with anxiety as she looked at him. He considered the tip of his cigar for a moment, then he asked abruptly: 'Has he a lot of money?'

A little puzzled frown marked her brow. 'Do you mean Philip or the doctor?'

'Well, I don't suppose the doctor has — yet!'

She glanced at him quickly.

'I — I don't understand — '

'Nothing,' he said disarmingly. 'Just the way my mind works.'

She sipped slowly at her brandy. 'It's odd you should say that,' she observed, over the rim of her glass. 'Philip inherited his uncle's fortune two or three months ago.'

'I see.'

'Our home's in South Africa,' she explained. 'Uncle was our guardian — and when he died Philip came to England. Several weeks ago I had a letter from Dr. Markham saying my brother had been taken ill and he was attending him in his nursing home. There was nothing to worry about, he said.'

Jimmy looked interested.

'Go on!'

'Then, a little later, Philip's solicitors in

London wrote.' Again a perplexed frown touched her brow. 'They were very disturbed because it seemed he was paying out large sums of money to various people. People I'd never heard of, and I'm sure Philip never knew before he came here. It was so disturbing I decided to come over and find out all about it.'

'Which, however, Dr. Markham seems anxious to prevent you from doing?'

'That's perfectly true!' She stared at him blankly. 'But how could you possibly know?'

'Merely a lucky guess.' He smiled at her and said easily: 'Since you and I are likely to be sharing each other's company for the next few hours, it might be cosier if I told you my name. I'm Jimmy Strange. I shan't raise the least objection if you call me 'Jimmy'; in fact I'd rather like it.'

Her eyes were bright, and a dimple appeared in her cheek which made his heart beat like a trip-hammer.

'I'm Sandra Carthew,' she said.

He said: 'Well, Sandra, the job we've got on our hands is to get your brother out of that — er — nursing home; and the sooner the better for his health and bank balance.'

She gave a shocked gasp. 'You mean you think they're ill-treating him — '

'Take it easy. Finish your drink while we think of ways and means. I'm going to help you. You can trust me.'

She looked up at him more calmly, and said softly:

'I think I can.'

'First we might look up our friend Dr. Markham and see what qualifications he has — if any — for running a nursing home.'

Some twenty minutes later she was looking over his shoulder as he flipped the pages of a medical directory in the local public library.

'Here we are,' he said, after a moment. 'Hmm . . . he's a doctor all right. Quite genuine.' He frowned thoughtfully. 'An alienist and specialist in mental disorders. All the bag of tricks. Address in Wimpole Street.' He turned to her with a dubious expression. 'Doesn't seem to be anything phoney there, I'm afraid. He appears to be on the level — ' He broke off as his eyes, returning to the directory, alighted on the date of the doctor's birth. He made a rapid calculation. 'Hello! Judging from this, Dr. Markham would be seventy-three.' He reflected a moment. 'And our man couldn't be a day over fifty.'

She nodded excitedly. Then said:

'Perhaps there are two Dr. Markhams?'

He was already checking the possibility.

'No, only this one.' A note of triumph was in his voice. 'I'll just make a note of the telephone number.' He scribbled it down. 'And go back to make a 'phone call.'

Her face was alight with excitement as she got into the car. Glancing at her beside him as he drove off, Jimmy realized, with a sudden sense of shocked guilt that he'd forgotten all about Gail, who was being borne farther and farther away in the Scots express. He tried to concentrate on Gail for a moment, but the girl at his side sabotaged every effort.

She joined him in the cramped telephone box at the inn, and he would not have been Jimmy Strange had he not been more than stirred by her proximity.

Finding it increasingly difficult to keep his mind on the job in hand, he gave the number and was answered by Dr. Markham's secretary.

'No, I'm afraid you can't speak to Dr. Markham. He left for America a month ago.'

'When will he be back?' What was the subtly haunting perfume the girl pressed close to him was wearing?

'Not for several months. He's giving a series of lectures over there.'

'I see.'

Jimmy hung up and said to Sandra: 'Our hunch is working along the right lines. He's an impostor sure certain.'

'You're really sure?'

'As sure as I am eggs don't bounce.'

'What are we going to do?'

Her look of helpless appeal aroused all his protective instincts. He wanted to take her in his arms there and then. Instead, he exerted great self-control and said: 'First of all I suggest we exhale sufficiently for us to extricate ourselves from this call box. Then maybe I can think up something.'

With her distracting influence more at arm's length he was able to concentrate with somewhat less difficulty. After a moment he returned to the 'phone-box and with a grin at her carefully shut himself in — alone. Within a minute or two a voice like a cross between a buzz saw and a foghorn was rasping in his ear.

'Hello, Crow, old bird. Strange as it may seem, Strange is the name!'

'So it's you,' Inspector Crow grunted in disgust.

'I hope I find you well?' Jimmy said sweetly.

'If you've rung up just to inquire after my health you could've saved yourself the money.'

Jimmy chuckled.

'Come on, what's biting you?' Crow exploded.

'My, my, you do sound bad-tempered. What is it, touch of liver?'

'You'll leave my liver alone.'

'Oh, I will, I will! All the same, I — er — think you should see a doctor about it.'

His expression registering mock horror and shocked disapproval, Jimmy held the receiver away from his ear as from it crackled a flow of English that was unprintably basic.

'And now will you tell me what you've got to say and then get the hell off the line!' finally roared the Inspector.

Imperturbably Jimmy observed: 'Matter of fact, there's a doctor down here who might do you quite a bit of good.'

Inspector Crow, his vocabulary temporarily exhausted, could only choke apoplectically. He ground his teeth. 'If you don't — !'

'Dr. Markham, he *calls* himself. Though it occurs to me you might know him better as Fisher. Max Fisher.' And half to himself he went on reflectively: 'I had a feeling at the back of my mind I'd seen the gentleman before . . . '

Crow's blustering roar had cut off like a door shutting out the sounds of a raging storm. In a deadly quiet tone he was saying: 'Max Fisher, did you say?'

Jimmy grinned into the mouthpiece.

'If you'd care for an appointment with him, well, I think it could be arranged for — shall we say ten o'clock tonight?'

The Inspector's only response was a grunt like that of a dyspeptic seal.

'Ten p.m. it is, then,' said Jimmy easily. 'At the dear doctor's nursing home. Now pin your big ears back, Beautiful, and let these following words of wisdom seep into that solid block of ivory you fondly imagine is your brain!' And ignoring the other's affronted bellowing, Jimmy proceeded smoothly to outline the plan of action he had been turning over in his mind. He spoke crisply, incisively. When finally he hung up he was chuckling softly to himself and there was an anticipatory gleam in his eyes.

★ ★ ★

The luminous dial of his wristwatch registered precisely twelve minutes to ten as Jimmy Strange paused alongside the tall hedge that ran for some forty yards along the narrow lane. Beside him stood Sandra, her eyes bright in the moonlight. She was very close to him, which was not surprising, considering that his arm had — in a purely protective gesture, of course — found its way round her slim waist. They had proceeded a few paces when she stopped suddenly.

'Look,' she said. 'You can see the house now. Through those trees.'

'We should find a gap in this hedge in a minute. Then, when the moon's covered by that cloud — '

'In we go!'

'You're not scared?' he smiled.

'It's exciting!'

You aren't exactly dull yourself! he thought, looking at her. He concentrated his attention on the project before them, and said: 'This looks the spot.'

'Yes, we can push through there all right.'

He led the way. 'Watch out for your face, some of these thorns are a bit aggressive.'

Negotiating a small orchard, they made their way cautiously towards the back of the nursing home. As the moon reappeared from behind the cloud they moved into the shadows of the house that loomed, dark and forbidding, before them. With a professional glance, Jimmy picked out a window and deftly forced the blade of a penknife against the catch. It snapped back and noiselessly he raised the sash.

Breathlessly Sandra watched him slip easily into the room.

'Stick around a moment,' he grinned at her. Then he had melted into the darkness.

Moving like a shadow, Jimmy made his way into the hall and quickly ascended a wide, dimly lit staircase. He calculated that Sandra's brother would be imprisoned in an upper room, and his immediate object was to locate it at once. As he reached the top of the staircase a burly white-coated figure moved towards him, away from the door he was obviously guarding. Jimmy recognized him as one of the plug-uglies he had encountered earlier with the fake doctor.

The man halted and stared at him, jaw sagging in astonishment. Before he could move into action or call out an alarm, Jimmy reached him with a punch that closed his sagging jaw with a snap. Without a sound the man slid to the floor, blissfully to dream away the next twenty minutes. Grabbing him by the collar, Jimmy dragged him into the room he had been guarding and shoved him into a corner. On the bed he found Philip Carthew lying in a drugged sleep.

Grim and purposeful, Jimmy went out, closing the door, and swiftly descended to the hall. As he re-crossed the hall he heard a car drive up outside the front door, its heavy wheels crunching on the gravel, its brakes squealing to a stop.

He glanced at his watch, a smile quirking the corners of his mouth. Ten o'clock and the ever-punctual Inspector Crow had arrived on the dot! Quickly he gained the dark room, and as he reached the window outside where Sandra was anxiously awaiting his return, a heavy peal on the doorbell shattered the stillness of the house.

It was prim, aesthetic-looking Sergeant Warburton, who was accompanying Crow, who had pulled the doorbell with a violence that had been quite unintentional. As the clanging reverberated within he murmured in some dismay: 'Dear me! I never meant to ring so loudly as that.'

Beside him Inspector Crow, his great chin deep in his coat-collar, grunted with heavy sarcasm: 'Trouble with you, Sergeant — you don't know your own strength.'

The door opened suddenly. Silhouetted against the dim light of the hall a man stood peering at them uncertainly.

'Good evening!' growled Crow, moving forward heavily. 'I believe this is — er — Dr. Markham's nursing home?'

The other stiffened. 'I am Dr. Markham. What is it you want?'

'Sorry to disturb you, but we're from Scotland Yard.'

There came a quick, involuntary gasp. 'Scotland Yard?'

'And I'm wondering if I could have a word with you, Doctor. I'm Detective-Inspector Crow.'

The man hesitated a moment, then said with complete composure. 'Why, certainly. Of course.' He held the door wide. 'Come in.'

'Thanks.' The Inspector glanced round at the police-car behind them. At the wheel a policeman sat, watchful, and another officer stood purposefully waiting. With a nod to Sergeant Warburton to follow him, Crow lumbered into the house. The door closed after them. The man who called himself Dr. Markham led them across the hall.

'Come into my consulting room. We can talk there.'

As they followed him, Sergeant Warburton sniffed delicately.

'Disinfectant,' he murmured. 'Quite the authentic atmosphere. Reminds me of when *I* was in hospital. Did I ever tell you about my operation, Inspector — ?'

'Shurrup!' rasped Crow. And, blushing slightly, the Sergeant subsided.

They entered the consulting room.

'Well, Doctor,' grunted the Inspector without any preamble, 'it's about a young woman.'

The other blinked at him behind his horn-rimmed glasses, and there seemed to be a note of relief in his voice. 'A young woman?'

'She disappeared from the hotel in the village near here where she's been staying.

We've — er — we've received information she was seen to enter this house. This evening it was — '

'*My* house?' The man was smiling blandly. 'What a preposterous suggestion! There's no female here, I can assure you, Inspector. I've no women patients or nurses either. The cook and cleaners are local women who leave at six o clock.'

'Quite so.'

Inspector Crow was comparing in his mind's eye the features of the man facing him with the police photographs of one Max Fisher. Photographs that he had been perusing recently. Grimly he decided that behind the horn-rims and probably dyed hair the individual before him might very easily be none other than Fisher. The same Max Fisher who had already served a sentence for posing as a medical man and running a bogus nursing home.

Satisfied on this point, Inspector Crow's beetling ginger brows drew together as he considered the neat little plan, evolved by Jimmy Strange, which was to show up the fake doctor within the next few minutes. That is, if the plan worked.

'I suppose,' the other was saying coolly. 'one of the yokels round here has been allowing his imagination to run riot. Eh, my dear Inspector?'

'Very possibly.' And Crow gave a surreptitious glance at the wall-clock opposite. Three minutes past ten. Things should start to happen any moment!

The little man was still talking. Talking expansively now, easily, with what might be a mocking smile in the eyes behind their horn-rimmed glasses. 'As a matter of fact, I rather fancy some of the villagers do regard me with some suspicion, don't you know. As an intruder and all that . . .'

Inspector Crow nodded absently, he was listening for another sound that would not be denied by the other's genial purr. He said with heavy formality: 'You'll appreciate, of course, we have to follow up anything which we think may need looking into.'

'Absolutely. But I'm afraid I can't help you.' He laughed as if enjoying a rich

30

joke. 'Sorry to disappoint you, but I've no disappearing girls on the premises!'

'I'm sure you're right.' said Crow, his ears hurting him, he was listening so tensely.

'Perhaps you'll have a drink before you go?' the other said, adding: 'and your colleagues too — '

At that moment a piercing scream tore through the house.

'Help! Help! Police! Help! Murder . . . '

For a second or two no one moved an inch in the consulting room. The Inspector's eyes gleamed triumphantly, Sergeant Warburton sucked in his breath, while the other stood as if thunderstruck, his mouth gaping wide open.

'Help! Police! Murder! Help! Police . . . '

The screams, *unmistakably those of a young woman*, came from somewhere upstairs.

Crow lumbered forward, his great jaw stuck out aggressively, and confronted the individual before him, whose mouth was now opening and closing like a fish out of water. 'What the hell?' he rasped. 'So you've got no females on the premises, eh?'

'I — I don't know. I tell you, I — '

'If that's not a girl screaming her head off, perhaps you'll kindly explain — with your superior medical knowledge — just exactly *what* it is!'

And Sergeant Warburton primly observed: 'It's a remarkably light voice for any *man* to have — even a very high tenor.'

'Shurrup!' Inspector Crow wheeled on him. 'Fetch the other officers and search the house. Move!'

'At once, sir,' said the Sergeant, and with another blush suffusing his pale features he hurried out. The Inspector turned on the other.

'Well, Dr. Markham, if that's who you are, are you going to give me your explanation now — or later?'

'I don't understand. I — I tell you, I'm as surprised — as puzzled as you are — '

'Not as puzzled as you're going to be trying to get out of these,' said Crow, with heavy humour, as he snapped the handcuffs over the man's wrists.

★　★　★

An hour or so later Jimmy's Strange's car was ticking over outside the 'Rainbow Inn'.

Philip Carthew had been conveyed there from the sinister nursing home in the care of a specialist hurriedly brought from London. Max Fisher — *alias* Dr. Markham — had confessed that he'd been systematically doping his victim into signing away large sums of money, but the Harley Street specialists pronouncement was that young Carthew would make a complete recovery and suffer no ill effects from the grim experience he'd undergone.

Jimmy came out of the inn, Sandra Carthew at his side. He reached the car and turned to take her hands in his. He said:

'Well, it's been fun knowing you.'

'It's been *wonderful* knowing you — Jimmy.'

'Wonderful is the word *I* had in mind, too,' he said gently.

'I'll never be able to thank you for all you've done,' she whispered.

'Think nothing of it,' he grinned. Then

his smile crooked a little as he looked into her eyes, soft and luminous in the moonlight. He gave a little sigh. He said with a reminiscent chuckle: 'Only one thing I'm sorry I missed tonight.'

'And what would that be?'

'The sight of Fisher's face when that scream hit his eardrums!'

She laughed.

He opened the door preparatory to getting into the car. Then he paused and regarded her with a quizzical look.

'Yes . . . ' he said slowly, 'you couldn't have screamed louder if someone had tried to kiss you.'

She seemed to be very close to him as she answered softly:

'Doesn't that depend on the 'some-one'?'

2

The Rose with a Thorn

The telephone beside Gresham's bed rang. With a frown he put down the novel he was reading and answered it. As he lifted the receiver he glanced at his wristwatch and noted the time. It was late for anyone to be 'phoning him.

'Hello?' And then his face turned ashen.

The voice in his ear was saying: 'Gresham . . . ? This is Lingley . . . ' With a soft chuckle, the voice went on: 'Remember me?'

'What — what d'you want?'

His effort to speak steadily was unconvincing, and there were beads of perspiration on his brow.

'As if you didn't know!' came the answer.

Gresham grasped the receiver so that his knuckles showed white. 'I can't pay you any more, I haven't got it — '

'A matter of a mere five thousand?' the

voice chided him. 'Come, come, my dear Gresham.'

'It's no good, I can't do it, I tell you. You've bled me white — '

Lingley cut in remorselessly:

'Unless I get the money by tomorrow . . . well — need we go into that painful subject again?'

'You swine! I can't — you know I can't — '

The other might not have heard. 'Twelve o'clock tomorrow. Goodbye.'

'No, no!' pleaded Gresham. 'I'll finish everything!' he shouted wildly. 'I'll shoot myself — '

The only reply was the click of the telephone being replaced at the other end. Desperately Gresham flashed his receiver up and down.

'Lingley! *Lingley* — '

He let his receiver fall into place with a hopeless groan. 'This is the finish . . . ' he muttered. Suddenly the hunted look gave place to one of desperation.

'The finish,' he repeated grimly. 'Yes, that's it. *The finish!*'

He pulled open the drawer of his

bedside table. His trembling fingers closed on a revolver. He looked at it, breathing heavily, then gave a sudden half-crazy exultant laugh.

'I'll escape him *this* way.' His voice rose. *'I'll escape him!'*

He placed the revolver to his head.

The echoes of the shot reverberated against the walls in ever-widening and fading echoes. Echoes that very soon were to reach the ears of Detective-Inspector Crow of Scotland Yard.

And, coincidentally enough, the ears of Jimmy Strange.

It was the following evening. A slack time at 'Joe's Place', that little dive in Greek Street, and the figure propping up the bar, his dress-shirt of impeccable whiteness and soft black hat tilted over one eye, was the solitary customer. Over his whisky he was glancing with idle amusement at the bartender scanning the racing results. The barman's face was sour, and with a grunt of disgust he turned the page.

'I'll never touch the blarsted nag again,' he grumbled. 'I tell yer if that son of a mule was in a race all by himself 'e'd still finish larst!'

Jimmy Strange raised his glass. 'Lost much?'

'Few quid.'

'Too bad.'

'Aw, I can't never get hold o' dough. Only time I ever did was when I was bustin' safes.' He sighed heavily. 'Even that didn't larst long, and they 'ad me bustin' rocks on Dartmoor.'

Jimmy said sympathetically: 'It's a hard life.'

'They was 'ard rocks,' the other ruminated reminiscently. Suddenly, as his gaze travelled down the page he had turned, his eyes narrowed. ' 'Ullo,' he said. 'Seen this?'

'What?'

' 'Ere, in the paper. Hugh Gresham has gorn and blowed 'is napper orf!

'Says here he's bin overworking.' He sniffed, then added: 'Well, 'e'll have a long holiday now!' Half to himself, he went on thoughtfully: 'Had enough of it, I suppose, that's wot.'

Jimmy glanced at him quizzically

through a cloud of cigarette smoke.

'Enough of it?'

'Bein' blackmailed, that's wot.'

Jimmy winced slightly. He said:

'Could you change the record and tell me exactly what is what?'

'I told yer. 'E 'ad the black on 'im, that's wo — '

'Quite,' Jimmy cut in quickly. He tapped the ash off his cigarette. 'I see,' he said softly. Then murmured casually:

'And who was the — er — ?'

'Yer mean the — ?'

'Yes.'

'Don'tcher know?'

The other glanced round the deserted saloon. Then leaned over the bar and, with one eye on the door, spoke from the corner of his mouth. 'Paul Lingley. Smooth 'un, 'e is.' He folded the newspaper and pushed it under the counter. 'They say the cops is wise to him, but 'e's too smart for 'em.'

'Umm?'

'That Rosie Lang, she works with him.'

Jimmy evinced the faintest flicker of interest. Rosie was, he knew, a singer at that nightclub of doubtful repute, the 'Black Lizard'. He said:

'Rose with a thorn, eh?'

'Pretty sharp, too!'

'Decoy duck?'

'And a pretty tough bird!'

'Sings nicely, though, doesn't she?'

'Search me. She don't wear much,' the barman leered.

'Haven't seen her lately, matter of fact. Maybe I should take another peek some time.' He contemplated his glass for a moment, then drained it and said half to himself: 'That's an idea. 'Night.'

' 'Night.' And added with a smirk: 'Hopes you like her — voice!'

The shadow of a smile flickered across his face, and with a touch at his black tie Jimmy Strange went out. The bartender watched him go with speculative eyes. He's either a crook or a dick, he decided. And yet he don't look like a cop. More likely a crook. One of them 'gentleman' sort.

So Rosie Lang was mixed up in the Gresham business, was she? mused Jimmy, as he made his way quickly down

Greek Street. He had, in fact, already given the newspaper report of the suicide a cursory glance in an earlier edition. 'Well-known Clubman's Tragic Death' and all the rest of it. It hadn't attracted his attention particularly. The activities of London's upper crust, whether they were running off with someone else's wife or taking a longer trip of the sort Gresham had bought himself a ticket for, didn't exactly cause him to miss any sleep.

But the introduction of the Lingley-plus-Rosie combination gave the setup a new angle. Nobody could accuse Jimmy of being narrow-minded, and his view of the manner in which certain members of society made a living was conditioned by his acquaintance with, and singularly omniscient knowledge of, the characters concerned and the sort of philosophy their social background had taught them.

Blackmail, though, was something else again.

While it would be ingenuous as well as highly inaccurate to describe the

41

majority of *habitués* of the underworld as moralizing sentimentalists, yet they, no less than law-abiding citizens, indicted blackmail, regarding its practitioners with, to put it mildly, implacable disfavour. Certainly, everyone from crooks to cops looked forward to the day when Lingley would get what was coming to him.

Though he was in no way against accelerating that happy day, and might even be disposed to putting in an oar of his own to that effect, nevertheless it is unlikely Jimmy Strange would have done much about it had it not been for Rosie's participation in the plot. There were plenty of nasty characters of the Lingley specifications around town. One more or one less out of action wouldn't add up to all that difference.

But Rosie — well, there weren't plenty of her around. Her blueprint was unique. He had first seen her at some low dive that had since been raided and closed by the police. She had sung her songs to the accompaniment of a tinny piano played by a chain-smoking semi-inebriate, and had still contrived to put herself over with an air and a style that obviously destined her for better things. It wasn't so much her numbers or even the way she delivered them. The goods she sold the customers was a dark sultry beauty of face, an outline that was definitely luscious plus a way of wearing a blatantly cheap sequin gown which made it look a million dollars.

Jimmy had been more than impressed by her, but had let it go for the simple reason he'd at once sensed Rosie spelled trouble for the poor fish who got entangled in her net. Trouble with a capital 'T'. Playing with fire wasn't one of Jimmy's forms of amusement on account of he knew burning your fingers spoiled their touch. He liked to think his touch was pretty sensitive, and he wanted it to stay that way.

Now, however, he visualized an opportunity of entering into a not-unexciting game with the pulchritudinous Rosie, assured that all the cards were stacked in his favour, with an ace or two up his sleeve just for luck. And incidentally he ought to do Lingley a bit of no good too. He recollected Rosie had in fact owed her present job to Lingley, who had an interest in the nightclub, and used to frequent the dive where she had first bloomed. She had reciprocated his attentiveness to the extent at any rate of letting him set her up in the more glamorous surroundings and commensurate financial attraction offered by the 'Black Lizard'.

As he turned into Shaftesbury Avenue his reflections were interrupted by the sight of a telephone-box on the corner. He paused, and his thoughts switched to a little job that had been occupying his mind for some days. He lit a cigarette and wondered whether or not this was a suitable moment to call a certain number named Sandra.

That was a someone he definitely planned to do something about. Since the 'Rainbow' episode he'd 'phoned her several times on the pretext of inquiring about the progress of her brother's convalescence. Over the 'phone she'd sounded warm and obviously interested in him, but her response was somewhat evasive regarding his idea that they should meet and get better acquainted. She felt the responsibility of her brother pretty heavily and Jimmy deduced that until Philip Carthew was fit to return to South Africa, which would not be for several weeks, she was going to be difficult to get close to. The closest he'd managed since the 'Rainbow' was her voice at the other end of a telephone, which wasn't his idea of close at all.

He was just deciding with some reluctance that as her brother was hardly at death's door, another call so soon after his solicitous inquiries of only the day before might seem redundant, when a voice said in his ear:

' 'Evening, Mr. Strange.'

He turned to regard the thin, ferrety-looking individual at his side. Giving him a friendly nod, he said:

'Nice to see you around again.'

'Thanks.' The other grinned, then said: 'If I had a cigarette I'd ask you to oblige with a light.'

Jimmy took out his case and flipped it

open, then lit his cigarette for him. The man inhaled long and luxuriously and muttered gratefully through a cloud of tobacco-smoke:

'I'd recommend you for a life-saving certificate,' he said, 'only what'd be the use of it? Now if they gave you a silver frame to go with it, that'd be something. But you only get the certificate.'

'So don't let's bother about it,' said Jimmy.

'Okay, we won't.' He eyed Jimmy's black tie and impeccable evening shirt with calculating appreciation.

'I see we are all dolled up to go places.'

Jimmy regarded him with a little chuckle. The ferret-faced one happened to be about the smartest jewel thief around town — though not smart enough to beat the twelve-months' sentence he'd just served — and his appraisal of the platinum evening-dress studs Jimmy was wearing was professionally automatic. Over the man's shoulder Jimmy said:

'If you're really interested in something in the tinfoil and paste line, take a look at that baby.'

The other glanced round as a smooth-purring limousine passed in which sat a stout character with a face bulging like a beetroot over his white tie beside a blonde dripping in jewellery. 'Lord and Lady Norvell,' he muttered sardonically, 'with her ladyship decked out in everything but the kitchen stove as per.'

His narrowed gaze followed the car as it swept on up Shaftesbury Avenue, and Jimmy could almost hear his mouth water as he added: 'And it ain't paste or tinfoil neither. Our little chorus-girl didn't marry the old buzzard for that!'

Jimmy said:

'I'll be moving.'

'Which way you going?'

'In the general direction of the 'Black Lizard', since you ask.'

The man shot him a quick look.

'Well . . . so long's your general direction don't take you inside the dump, you'll keep your nose clean.' And then: 'Or is all this fancy dress in aid of Rosie Lang?'

'Curious, or d'you just want to know?'

'Curious.'

'Why so?'

'No particular reason. After all, she curves where she should and you won't be the first to want to wrap it up and take it home.'

'Following in Gresham's footsteps, eh?'

'You read the newspapers, too.'

'The bits that don't have the big words.'

The other squinted at him sideways and grinned knowingly. He said: 'I wouldn't be wasting my breath, would I, Mr. Strange, tipping you off about Rosie Lang?'

Jimmy smiled at him amiably.

'You have very nice thoughts,' he murmured, 'and I'm sure you mean well.'

'P'raps you'll put that in writing? I can show it the cops next time I'm pinched.'

'I sincerely hope there'll be no next time.'

'Do my best for you. Anyway, don't put anything in writing for Rosie. She'll only pass it on for someone else to read. But you've heard about him, too, I shouldn't wonder.' And with another knowing grin he moved off.

Jimmy watched him abstractedly until

his thin sidling figure had disappeared. There was a glint of anticipatory amusement in his eyes as he crossed Shaftesbury Avenue and continued on his way.

Rosie was in the middle of her show when he arrived and he sat down and gazed at her over his drink with the appreciation of a connoisseur.

He thought she looked more attractive than when he'd seen her before. She'd acquired a blatant take-it-or-leave-it style of salesmanship that lent the trite lyrics she sang a kind of saltiness and lifted her performance well out of the general run of cabaret moaner. Yes, she'd come a long way since the Soho dive. The sequined affair she was wearing, which sparkled in the spotlight and left practically nothing whatsoever to the imagination, was no cheap job. She really was an eyeful of allure.

Looking round, Jimmy got the idea in a general way the customers were eating her up. He attracted a waiter's eye, ordered another drink and relaxed. He told himself he was looking forward to meeting Rosie.

When later on he introduced himself to her in her dressing room he got it at once that his complimentary remarks were met with a certain amount of suspicion. He calculated he wasn't exactly the type of admirer she wanted around admiring. There was nothing of the tired business-man about him. Instinctively she was picking up a wavelength that was warning her he wasn't there strictly for the benefit of her health.

She stared at his reflection in the brightly lit mirror before her with hard, speculative eyes.

'It's nice of you to say all these nice things,' she said, retouching her eyelashes already heavy with mascara. Then her voice grew hard. 'But you didn't call just to tell me what a great artist I am — or did you?'

'No?' he queried, with a disarming smile. 'Perhaps you're right.'

She turned and stared at him.

'Who the devil are you?'

The smile became enigmatic. 'Oh, let's not go into that now.' Then, with elaborate casualness, he said: 'Seen tonight's paper?'

Suddenly she faced him.

'Listen,' she said. 'I don't know who you are, but just clear out, see?'

His gaze travelled over her with undisguised admiration. He said: 'Clever of you to have got Gresham write you those letters.'

It caught her clean off her guard. 'I never thought he'd kill himself,' she blurted out, then stopped short.

'Don't suppose you did. Any more,' he went on easily, surveying the glowing tip of his cigarette, 'than you've thought about the possibility of Lingley finishing with you.'

'What *are* you yapping about?'

'Just that I've an idea you're going to meet with — an accident.'

She laughed disbelievingly. 'Don't be so dumb!'

But her eyes were not smiling. There was a baffled expression in them. What he had said had shaken her. He seemed to know an awful lot, she was telling herself. How, she couldn't guess, but he knew. Even more than she did, it suddenly struck her with apprehension, because he was insinuating that Lingley ... A thought occurred to her.

'You trying to scare me?'

'No. Merely explaining that you know too much.' He sighed regretfully. 'However ... '

Suddenly she felt frightened.

But she knew all right why Gresham had shot himself that Lingley had driven him to it. She knew all about it — hadn't she been in on the blackmail plot? The letters she'd got the old fool to write her and everything. His suicide had come as a terrible shock to her. She had never considered the possibility of a thing like that. Lingley, on the other hand, had been quite unconcerned, complaining cynically what a nuisance it was he would have to find another mug to work on.

Yes. he was pretty tough, Lingley. The question rose up in her mind. Would he be capable of ... ? She didn't frame the rest of it in words; she suddenly felt a chill of foreboding. She forced a derisive smile to her lips.

'You're talking through your hat,' she said.

He had been watching her closely. Now, with a casual shrug, he turned away. He moved to the window, gazing idly down into the street. 'Maybe,' he said, over his shoulder. 'May — ' He broke off, his body stiffening.

'What's the matter?'

Without looking at her he said in a flat voice: 'Come over here by the window. See that chap down there in the shadow?'

She gave a quick gasp. 'Why — why, yes — '

He said, with elaborate nonchalance: 'Been hanging around quite awhile.'

'Who — who is he?'

He didn't answer for a moment. She glanced at him and saw that his jaw had set in a grim line. Then: 'One of Lingley's boys,' he said.

She was visibly shaken. Turning away from the window, he said quietly: 'Still think I'm talking through my hat?'

Her answer was written in her face.

'Oh God . . . ' she whispered. 'He warned me that if ever I played him any tricks, he'd — he'd — ' She broke off.

'He'd what?'

'Have me taken care of!'

Jimmy nodded. 'And he doesn't sound the sort who'd break a promise to a lady.' He took her arm and led her away from the window.

He said: 'Now, wouldn't you like to see him put away for a long time?'

She shook her head. 'He's too smart.'

'Not too smart for you and me,' he grinned at her. 'We could fix him. Why not lend a hand?'

She hesitated while he watched her narrowly through a cloud of cigarette smoke. The baffled look had returned to her eyes. She was trying hard to figure out who he was and all about him. What was his line? How did he know so much? And why had he chosen to come and see her like this? A dozen questions were on her lips, and then she saw the ghost of a smile flicker across his face. He was reading her thoughts, and she realized her questions wouldn't get her very far. She looked at him, her eyes narrowed with speculation. There was something about his quiet, casual attitude that gave her a sudden feeling of confidence in him. She glanced at the window and a shiver ran down her spine.

She made up her mind.

'All right. I'm on your side.'

'Meet me tomorrow, one o'clock, the Regis Grill, and we'll arrange the whole thing.' He picked up his hat. 'Bye-bye for now.'

She stopped him with a movement. 'But what about the man outside?'

'Don't worry,' he said easily. 'Leave him to me.'

And he was gone.

A few moments later he approached a man who was lounging in the shadow of a doorway, his shoulders hunched and hands thrust deep into pockets.

'All right, old chap,' he said briskly, 'you can push off now.'

'Yes, guv'nor. Everything okay?'

Jimmy chuckled softly. 'Fine,' he said. 'You looked most sinister from that window!' He pressed a note into the man's grimy hand. 'Here, get yourself a drink.'

'Coo, thanks, guv'nor. Nice pay for just standing about for arf an hour!' He touched his hat and slouched off, muttering to himself: 'Blimey, money for jam!'

With an amused smile Jimmy Strange watched him go. Then he lit a cigarette and, turning, he walked quickly away and was swallowed up in the night.

Next day at the Regis Grill, Rosie was only ten minutes late, which indicated she was anxious to keep the appointment. When she arrived, Jimmy saw with pleasurable surprise that she was remarkably pretty — even more than she'd looked last night. Now her curvaceous figure and slimly tapering legs were less revealingly displayed than they'd been at the 'Black Lizard', her face was given more chance to attract the eye. Jimmy realized that from this new angle she was really lovely to look at.

He prepared to enjoy lunch.

His only serious contribution to the conversation was made over the coffee and liqueurs. He drew at his cigarette, blew a spiral of smoke ceilingwards, and leaned forward. He said:

'Now, Rosie, the plan I've figured out is simple . . . For you it's child's play — all you have to do is inform Lingley that you've hooked a rich jeweller.'

She gave him a puzzled look. 'But I don't know any jewellers.'

He smiled at her. 'You know me.'

Rosie eyed him with a new interest. 'You a jeweller?'

'To please Mr. Lingley, yes.'

'Oh . . . ' Then she said: 'A rich one?'

'Very.'

She sipped her Benedictine. 'Something tells me I'm going to like you, Jimmy!'

He grinned, then his mouth tightened. He said: 'Listen. You kid Lingley along. You let him know I'm the married and respectable type.'

'And are you?' she smiled at him.

'Am I what?'

'Married and respectable.'

'Cut the comedy for now,' he said, 'and pin your pretty ears back.' He paused a moment, then went on: 'If you do your stuff our friend will come on the scene to inform me it'll cost me a thousand to stop the letters reaching my wife. Are you with me?'

She nodded understandingly. 'I can see the wheels going round.'

'I agree to pay,' Jimmy continued. 'He fixes a meeting and I'm to bring the money.'

'And all the time you've got the busies hidden behind the aspidistra,' she said brightly, 'armed with recording apparatus.'

'You've been reading penny dreadfuls, my angel!' he chuckled. 'We take things a little less crudely in real life.' His smile became enigmatic, and he finished his liqueur. 'Expect the first love-letter from me tomorrow,' he said. 'And don't get ideas if it happens to be a sizzler!'

Some couple of weeks later a lean-faced man in a neat lounge suit gave a casual glance at a newspaper placard which billed some sensational jewel robbery, stepped into a call-box and rang Scotland Yard, asking for Detective-Inspector Crow.

'That you, Crow, old bird?'

The noise at the other end might have been an apoplectic bull.

'Who the hell — '

'Strange is the name' — sweetly. 'How d'you do?'

'You again!'

'You don't sound very pleased. Come, come, my dear Inspector . . . where's that unfailing courtesy of our London police we read so much about?'

Crow choked. 'Listen, you — get off the line — I'm busy.'

'Never mind,' Jimmy murmured laconically. '*I've* heaps of time.'

'Who the blazes d'you think you're talking to?'

'The most charming man at the 'Yard',' Jimmy said promptly. 'Am I right?' The choking sounds grew more violent, and he went on lightly: 'Just as I thought! Well, now, I'd like to tell you something about a certain character named Lingley — '

The other cut in with an abrupt change of tone: 'Lingley? What d'you know of him?'

'Just that you can pinch him — tonight.'

'Uh?'

'At the Star Hotel, that dump in Soho Street. First floor back you'll find him, *and* some rather interesting evidence.'

'Really?' said Crow, in affectedly bored tones. 'And what would you like me to do about it?'

Jimmy smiled to himself. He was not deceived by the Scotland Yard man's pretended disinterest.

'Listen,' he said. 'At ten o'clock someone'll come out of the hotel with a bit of a cough — like this.' He coughed with sudden racking violence into the telephone. He broke off to grin as Crow recoiled from the noise against his eardrum with a roar of protest.

'Stop that row; blast you!'

'Glad you like it. When this chap's gone — and it's essential you mustn't stop him, the whole thing depends on that — when he's gone you walk in and do your stuff. That's all.'

'Thank you very much for your kind information,' the Inspector said with heavy sarcasm.

'Pleasure, I'm sure. Will you be there?'

The other's reply was over-elaborately non-committal. 'I — er — might happen to be in that neighbourhood. I sometimes take a stroll there — '

Jimmy chuckled and rang off.

Shortly before ten o'clock he was speaking in appropriately aggrieved tones to a dark individual with soft pudgy hands. For his assumed role of the rich and errant husband lured from marital fidelity by an attractively young face and figure he wore horn-rimmed spectacles and a hangdog expression.

'Well, Mr. Lingley,' he was saying, 'there you are. Stiff price to have paid for a few silly letters.'

'I agree,' said the other smoothly. 'But then, letter-writing can be an expensive hobby.'

'So it seems.' A heavy sigh. 'You'll find those pearls worth a good thousand.'

Lingley nodded. 'I'm sure.'

He eyed the necklace with visible satisfaction, holding it up to admire its lustrous beauty. He smiled inwardly and only with difficulty abstained from smacking his lips. There would be plenty more from where these had come, he promised himself. The poor fool had his letters back all right — but not before he'd made photographic copies of them. Yes, he ought to be able to milk the mug for plenty.

Jimmy went on: 'Anyway, it was impossible for me to have got the cash at such short notice. Nor without causing great inconvenience and risking awkward questions being asked.'

'I'm quite satisfied, my dear sir,' the other purred.

Jimmy drew himself up in an attitude of repugnance. 'In that case,' he said with pomposity, 'perhaps you will excuse me?' He glanced at his watch. The expression he wore was exactly befitting that of a respectable businessman who has just concluded an unpleasant but necessary transaction without loss of dignity.

'Goodbye,' he said.

Alone with the necklace, Lingley fingered the pearls caressingly. He could hardly be blamed for omitting to notice that his departing victim was suddenly overcome by a paroxysm of coughing.

The coughs receded, to be replaced after a brief interval by the sound of hurriedly approaching footsteps. There came an imperative rap on the door that jerked Lingley's head up.

'Who's there?' he gasped, as a large, formidable and bowler-hatted figure stood in the doorway. Behind the visitor loomed another, somewhat more aesthetic in appearance and wearing a look of prim disapproval.

Quickly recovering his composure, Lingley said: 'Why, good evening, Inspector!' adding with an urbane smile directed towards Sergeant Warburton: 'I see you've brought a friend.'

Crow grunted, 'Hello, Lingley.' Then his bushy eyebrows shot up and he cut in quickly: 'Here, what you putting in your pocket?'

'Why, I — '

'Come on, let's have a look. Pearls, eh?'

'A little present from someone, my dear Inspector.'

The detective examined the necklace closely. 'Double row, graduated, emerald clasp . . . ' He looked up with an acid smile. 'You'll be telling me Lady Norwell herself gave 'em to you.'

Lingley stared at him in blank inquiry. 'What d'you mean?'

Warburton permitted himself a mirthless snigger.

'As if you didn't know!'

Crow scowled at him, and he blushed slightly. The Inspector said to Lingley: 'I only mean these were taken from Lady Norwell's safe early this morning.'

'What!'

'You can save your surprise for the jury.'

'This is outrageous!' Lingley blustered, his face livid. 'You can't do this!'

'I've been waiting to do it for a long time.'

'I tell you, I don't know — '

'Oh, come on, do,' murmured Sergeant Warburton petulantly. 'You're making the Inspector vexed!'

* * *

Some time later over a supper-table at a quiet little restaurant, Jimmy Strange was smiling:

'And that is the end of our dear Mr. Lingley.'

Rosie's lovely eyes were bright with undisguised admiration.

'Yes . . . ' Jimmy went on, 'he's going to be put away for a long time to come. Because he just can't explain how he came by Lady Norwell's very expensive string of pearls. That is unless he cares to admit they were paid to him in lieu of blackmail money. Which would really hardly help him at all!'

Rosie put her hand across the table. Her fingers touched his.

She said softly: 'You know, Jimmy, I could fall for you . . . '

He glanced down at her crimson fingernails and returned their pressure with suitable ardour.

He said: 'You know, Rosie, I could fall for you, too.'

'Let's take the dive together!'

He grinned at her. Yes, she was most attractive.

'The only thing,' he said, 'is that I'm such a susceptible chap and might fall harder than you. And I bruise so easily!'

'I wouldn't hurt you.'

'I wonder . . . '

He drew at his cigarette and looked at her through the smoke.

She realized that he was going to be even tougher to get than she'd anticipated. She said casually — a trifle too casually, he thought:

'By the way, you never told me who did pinch the pearls.'

A little enigmatic pause. Then he said easily: 'Need we go into that?' He found the waiter and turned to her. 'Time to take you home . . . You could persuade me in the taxi how painless falling for you really is.'

He was smiling at her as he said it, but he was thinking Sandra wouldn't have asked him that leading question. Something was telling him the danger about her would be a cosier kind than the danger he read at the back of Rosie's eyes.

There'd be no burning his fingers over Sandra and spoiling their touch. Which was all right with him on account of he regarded his touch as nice and sensitive and he liked it to stay that way.

3

The Man from the River

Tonight the river was a graveyard.

Someone was being buried without mourners. Below the hulls of the ships a blurred circle of light traced the progress of the furtive hearse, a slow-moving motorboat. Its engine made a muffled chugging as it cleaved the mist swirling over the black waters. Somewhere a distant tug-siren moaned.

Aboard the motorboat a heavy-shouldered man blew on his fingers. 'Damned cold,' he grumbled.

'Be colder for 'im,' his companion, a weedy little individual, nodded towards the huddled shape which lay inert in the stem. 'Pore blighter!' he added with a sniff.

The other grunted. 'Too sentimental, that's your trouble.'

The little man scratched his head.

'P'raps I am.' He glanced at the stern and shivered. 'I know I'll be glad when it's all over. Don't like it. Don't like it a bit.'

He strained his eyes through the shrouding mist as he handled the rudder. They seemed to be clear of the ships riding at anchor.

'We've come far enough,' said the big man. 'Turn midstream.'

'Not on your ruddy life!'

'Why not?'

'Never find our way back, not in this fog.'

'Who says we wouldn't?'

'I do.'

'Scared of getting lost, eh?' sneered the big man. 'Thought you said yer could find yer way round this part blindfolded — '

He broke off. The note of a deep hooter echoed. The sound of powerful engines was rapidly approaching. His companion stood tensely listening.

'Wot's that?' he whispered hoarsely.

'Wot?'

'River Perlice!' The other gulped with terror as he recognized the unmistakable note of the engine. 'I told yer it was too risky. They've spotted us!'

Panic-stricken, he snapped out the light and cut the motor. Cursing, the big man lurched forward, shoving him aside, and switched the light on again. As he restarted the engine, the light from the patrol boat swung in their direction. Deliberately he swivelled his lamp towards the oncoming vessel.

'Ahoy there!' came a hail from the police boat.

'Now you've done it,' muttered the little man. 'Switching the light on. Arsking for trouble — '

'Shut yer trap! I'll manage this.' He cupped his hands to his mouth. 'Ahoy!' he shouted back.

'All right there?' came from the patrol.

'Okay here, thanks.'

The beam from the police-boat swung off them, its engines revved and it disappeared into the mist. The little man gasped with relief and wiped the sweat off his face. His companion chuckled.

'Gone! If they'd found us without lights and no engine running, they'd have been aboard in a jiffy, And found him.' He scowled at the crumpled heap in the stern. He blew on his fingers, then went on in a self-satisfied tone: 'I'll give you a tip. When you're caught in suspicious circumstances, don't act suspicious. Be casual. Bluff 'em. Look out!' With a sudden exclamation he grasped the rudder. 'You'll run inter that ship. What the 'ell d'yer think you're doing?'

'I couldn't 'elp it. Fair shook me up, them cops did — me nerves ain't what they were.' His voice rose to a whine. 'I wish I'd never started this. We'll get pinched, I know we — '

The other gave him a sudden back-hander across his face that rattled his teeth.

'Now what d'yer know?'

The little man whimpered. 'Me nerves ain't what they were. I tell yer — '

'Shut up!'

He subsided. Then, with a touch of defiance muttered: 'But I ain't taking the boat midstream. Too risky, in all this fog. We might run into a ship, or — '

'Fat lot o' use you and your damned

boat turned out to be. I'd have done better if I'd pitched the body over the wharf. And saved me money.'

'I wish you 'ad.' Cutting the engine, he said obstinately: 'It'll be all right here. Deep enough, even at low water.'

The big man grunted impatiently. 'Come on, then.' He tied the rudder. 'Enough of this messing about; let's get 'im over, quick.'

'You take his feet, then.'

They shifted the body, lifting it on to the edge of the boat.

'Sure you tied those weights all right?'

The little man nodded.

'We don't want him to come up and float — '

'Don't worry — he'll stay down.'

'Here goes.' The big man gave a shove. 'Pleasant dreams!'

There was a heavy splash. Water spattered into their faces.

'Phew! That's that,' the little man breathed. 'Thank God.'

'Food for fishes,' the other chuckled, and revved the engine. 'Sure you fixed those weights so they wouldn't come off?'

he demanded again.

His companion sneered. 'You'd be worried if I hadn't, wouldn't you?'

The big man glowered at him for a moment, then he muttered between his teeth: 'And so will you have something to worry about if he don't stay down there!'

He swung the rudder. The motorboat chugged off, disappearing into the mist, its wake feathering behind, and then the river was black and smooth again.

* * *

Jimmy Strange was, in company with a number of others, propping up the bar of 'Joe's Place' in Greek Street.

'Joe's Place' is a rendezvous for as comprehensive a cross section of society as you could wish to meet. Also the drink's good. It is patronized by the sporting fraternity, the acting profession, journalists, and others whose occupations might be somewhat difficult to describe.

At 'Joe's Place' tipsters and ex-jockeys rub shoulders with confidence men and shady self-styled financiers. Flat-nosed boxers and gamblers raise elbows alongside cardsharpers and others who live by their wits at the expense of their more credulous fellows. Jimmy, his eye ranging casually over the noisy, smoke-misted gathering, was familiar with the pasts of most of them. He could also, without much difficulty, estimate the possibilities their futures held. That flashy-looking gentleman over there in evening clothes, for instance, was so smart he would end inevitably in outsmarting himself. That loud-mouthed character looking like a bookmaker, and in reality a 'fence', was destined to receive a long stretch of imprisonment because he talked too much.

Jimmy's gaze now rested ruminatively on a good-looking pale young man who'd come into the bar only a few moments before. He sat perched on a stool, soft hat on the back of his head, reading an evening paper. His name was Fowler, and he was an actor. He drained his drink as Jimmy moved over to him.

'Haven't seen you around for some time. What goes on?'

His soft voice with the curious metallic edge to it brought the young man's head up with a jerk.

'Nothing much good, I'm afraid.'

'Too bad. Have a drink; you'll feel better.'

'That's nice of you. It's a brandy-and-soda.'

Jimmy gave the order to the barman, adding a Scotch for himself.

He grinned sympathetically at the young man, and said:

'What's the trouble?'

'This and that.' His drink appeared before him, and he moved the brandy-glass in little circles over the bar. ' 'Matter of fact, I've had rather an unpleasant experience.'

Jimmy made a commiserating sound over his whisky.

'Been to a mortuary down by the river.'

'Good lor'!'

'Had to identify my father.' The other pulled at his lower lip. 'He was lugged out this morning.'

Jimmy said: 'Drowned, you mean?'

The other passed his newspaper. 'Here,

read that.' He pointed shakily to an item on the front page.

Jimmy read:

RIVER MYSTERY. MAN'S BODY FOUND. POLICE INVESTIGATE.

Two schoolboys fishing from a boat off Wharfside this morning made a gruesome discovery when their line became entangled in what they first thought were weeds. Further examination revealed that their fishing tackle was in fact hooked to the body of a man. The boys informed the authorities, who recovered the body. The man has been identified as Richard Fowler, of Park Mansions, Hammersmith. Certain features of the discovery have led to Scotland Yard being called in . . .

Then Jimmy gave a little smile to himself as he caught the name of the detective-inspector who was in charge of the case. He folded the paper thoughtfully and returned it to Fowler. He said:

'Your father, eh?'

'Yes.'

After a moment, Jimmy said slowly: 'And what were the 'certain features' that brought the police on the scene?'

'He'd been shot in the head and weights had been tied to him so's he wouldn't float.'

'Is that so?'

'I — can't understand it,' young Fowler puzzled. 'Oh, Dad was a no-good all right, I know — but who'd want to murder him?'

There was a little pause.

'Didn't you once tell me he was gambling crazy?' Jimmy said.

'I suppose he was, yes. He was a bit weak — easily led. He'd got mixed up with a fellow called Fenner — '

'Fenner, eh?'

The other man looked up quickly. 'You know him?'

'I've heard of him.'

Jimmy's answer was accompanied by a casual shrug. But there was a thoughtful look in his eyes as he ran his finger round the rim of his glass.

'I've heard of him, too. I warned Dad against him.'

'Did you, now?'

'He had a gambling joint. It was supposed to be run crooked.'

'Magnets, loaded dice, marked cards — usual set-up?'

'Something like that. But the Old Man wouldn't listen. Then I went out on tour with a show — just finished with it, I have. While I was away, Dad wrote me he and Fenner were starting some new place together. I didn't like that.'

He broke off as a thought struck him. 'I wonder if he . . . '

Jimmy was eying him narrowly. He said: 'Who — Fenner?'

'Yes. I wonder if — ' He shook himself. 'But that's ridiculous. I'm suspecting Fenner of murder, but why should he?'

Jimmy continued to regard him. Then: 'As you say, why should he?'

Fowler lifted his glass. 'Anyway, I've told the police all I know, so it's up to them now.'

'That's it. Wonderfully efficient organization, the police. Need a little encouragement now and then and a bit of friendly advice, but who doesn't?'

Having expressed these glib sentiments, Jimmy glanced at the empty glasses. The other took his cue.

'How about another one?'

'Mine's a Scotch.' He looked at his watch and added: 'Then I must be hopping it. Got another bar waiting for me to lean against.'

He drained the drink almost as soon as it was set on the counter and bade Fowler a hurried goodbye. Outside he hailed a taxi.

'Where to, sir?' asked the cabby. Then he shot Jimmy a look of recognition. 'Good evening, Mr. Strange.'

'Hello, Bert.' Jimmy in turn recognized him as one of several taxi drivers who habitually plied the Soho area and to whom he was known as a handsome tipper. 'How's the old asthma?'

'Mine, sir, or me taxi's?' grinned Bert, with an affectionate glance at his somewhat decrepit-looking cab.

'Both of you.'

'We still manage to wheeze our way

round, though we ain't as nippy as we used ter be. Still, we gets there just the same. Which reminds me, where shall we drop yer?'

''Mirrobar'.'

'Yessir.'

'By the way . . . ' Jimmy paused as he was about to get into the taxi, an idea striking him. 'Know the 'Starboard Light'?'

'Yer mean the pub, Wapping way?'

Jimmy nodded. 'You can collect me in twenty minutes and take me down there. Little business call I want to pay. But the 'Mirrobar' first.'

'Pleasure before business — that the idea, sir?' Bert grinned at him.

'What do you think?'

'I don't, sir. I just drives me taxi.'

At the 'Mirrobar' in Jermyn Street, Sandra greeted Jimmy with a quizzical smile. She was alone at a little table by the mirrored wall, and as he went over to her he correctly interpreted her look and quickly took the words from her lovely mouth.

'I know, I know. For someone who's

been saying he could hardly wait to see you, I'm just a trifle late.'

Her glance was cool, and she raised an exquisitely pencilled eyebrow at the gilt clock over the bar.

'And what, if the answer isn't too unexpected, would be your idea of a trifle?' she said.

'Need we quibble over that?'

'I see.' She looked him over carefully. 'And are you always going to let me hang around for ten minutes before you show up?'

'Is that in the nature of a threat or a promise?'

She didn't answer him at once. She contemplated him as if seeing him for the first time. Indeed, it was the first time since the meeting at the 'Rainbow'. She tried to analyze her reaction to him, and found the going extremely difficult. He was attractive all right — he attracted her, and at first glance that was easily explained. He was nice-looking, amusing. But so were plenty of other men she knew. Aside from the fact he had got her brother out of a very sticky jam she felt a warmth towards him. She liked being with him; Why he more than anyone else she didn't know.

He was ordering drinks from the waiter, and she caught the odd granite-like quality in his profile. She realized he was tough all right; yet when he looked at her, when he gave her that smile of his, the hardness vanished, the odd bleakness in his eyes went and was replaced by something that at moments made her catch her breath.

While she knew all these things, she was conscious that most of all he was elusive as a shadow. Was it, she wondered, that indefinable air of mystery about him which gave him the extra something the others hadn't got?

'D'you know,' she said, 'you haven't told me what you do.'

The waiter was placing their drinks before them, and he didn't reply until the man had gone. Then over his glass he said:

'Apart from keeping you waiting, you mean?'

'Apart from keeping me waiting, I mean.'

He smiled at her.

'Spend the rest of my time trying not to,' he said.

'Not to what?'

'Keep you waiting,' he said.

'You must be a busy man,' she said.

He shrugged. 'My day varies.'

'And the evenings?'

He looked at her thoughtfully for a moment. 'Depends.'

'You don't mind my asking questions?'

'Don't mind what you ask, so long's you stay right where you are and go on looking the way you do.'

'Now you've got me all confused,' she said.

'I feel that way about you, come to think.'

'I was going to ask you something, and I've forgotten what it was.'

'It'll come to you,' he said.

She shook her head. 'Something tells me you're the evasive type, anyway.'

He grinned at her non-committally.

'Tell me,' he said, as he lit her cigarette and then his own, 'you aren't going back to South Africa with your brother — or are you?'

'Haven't made up my mind.'

'When's he sail?'

'In two or three weeks.'

'Leaves you a little time to think it over,' he said.

She'd expected him to register a certain disappointment at the prospect of her going away. Any other man would surely have made some attempt to persuade her to stay, she reflected. But he just smiled at her casually through a cloud of cigarette smoke. Impossible to read what was going on behind that unfathomable gaze.

At that precise moment Jimmy was, as a matter of fact, searching his mind for an excuse with which he could tear himself away from Sandra's delightful presence. Mentally he cursed the fates for running him into Fowler and the story of his father's sinister death. Why couldn't he leave it alone, he asked himself, and let Scotland Yard do some work for a change? Here he was all set nice and easy with the one girl he'd wanted to be with more than anyone he'd ever known, and his attention was wandering to that other odd business.

From the tail of his eye he saw by the gilt clock that the faithful Bert would be drifting in for him in the next couple of minutes or so. How the hell would he explain it to Sandra? Even as he made another attempt to rack his brain for the answer, she leaned across and with a nod towards the door behind him said:

'Someone seems to be looking for you.'

Jimmy turned as Bert bore down on them, grinning genially.

'Well 'ere we are, Mr. Strange,' he wheezed.

'Hello, Bert. What's wrong?' Jimmy said, giving the other a quick wink.

The old cabby reacted with typical Cockney resource and nimble-wittedness. With a look at Sandra, on whom he bestowed a fatherly smile, he shook his head sadly at Jimmy and said:

'Business, I'm afraid, Mr. Strange.'

'Whose business?'

'Afraid you'll 'ave ter make it yours,' was the response, followed by more head-shaking.

Jimmy glanced at Sandra in well-simulated puzzlement, and she, as yet unacquainted with the fact that nothing ever surprised him or took him unawares, accepted it at its face value.

'They told me where I'd find yer,' went on Bert, vaguely dramatic, but so, nevertheless, effective, Jimmy could hardly restrain from applauding him. 'And said I was ter fetch yer.'

'You mean . . . ?' queried Jimmy, with a mysterious frown and entering into the spirit of the game he had started off.

'Exactly, Mr. Strange,' said Bert emphatically.

Jimmy turned to a completely bewildered Sandra, and his heart smote him for the deception he was so brazenly putting across. But he had to carry it off now.

'Afraid,' he said, with a smile of wonderfully contrived wryness, 'I must toddle.'

'But — ?'

'Hell, I know,' he said, 'but — ' He broke off with an eloquent shrug. 'I'll fix the waiter to get you a taxi to take you back home, and I'll 'phone you there soon's I can.' He stood up. Bert contributed one more histrionic gem to his performance by muttering hoarsely:

'Sorry ter break up the little *tête-à-tête*, miss, but Mr. Strange is at the beck and call of his — er — chief, as yer might say. Ain't that right, sir?'

Jimmy nodded with great seriousness. 'You might say I am,' he murmured.

And with another whimsical smile for her benefit he followed Bert, speaking a word to the waiter on his way, and was gone.

'You shocking old humbug,' he muttered at Bert's broad back as they went out. 'I don't know how the devil I'd have made out without you.'

Some twenty minutes later he pushed through the swing doors of the 'Starboard Light'. The saloon bar of the old waterfront tavern was smoke-fogged and acrid with tobacco smoke.

An untidy man with a heavy walrus moustache was guffawing explosively. His rolled-up sleeves proclaimed him to be the Proprietor, despite the fact that he was on the customers' side of the bar. He was leering bawdily at a bunch of cronies who were crowding round him for the pay-off on an anecdote: ' . . . And so she says to 'im, she says; 'Well, you might take yer 'at orf to a lady'!'

The roar of laughter was almost drowned by the storyteller's own bellowing guffaw. 'Lucky' Mallory always enjoyed his jokes more than his listener's did.

Jimmy pushed into the group. ' 'Evening, 'Lucky'!' he greeted. 'What's the comedy?'

'Lumme, if it ain't Mr. Strange!' He showed broken, tobacco-stained teeth. 'Well, this is a pleasant surprise!'

'Glad to see you, too. How's everything?'

'Quiet. sir. Very quiet.' He beckoned Jimmy aside and added in a whisper: 'Least, it was.' He winked. 'Trust you to smell out a bit of trouble.'

Jimmy laughed. 'I'm here because I'm thirsty.'

'For wot? Whisky — or — knowledge?'

'Both.'

'Lucky' pulled at his moustache. 'If

yer'd like ter come through to the back room you can 'ave yer drink there.'

He led the way through the bar, speaking over his shoulder. 'As a matter of fact, Mr. Strange, I don't mind telling yer things *ain't* bin so quiet — '

'You don't say?'

The other closed the door behind him. 'Pulled a body out of the wet, they did, this morning.' 'Lucky' was watching closely to see how much this information was worth.

Jimmy pointedly stifled a yawn and lounged into a creaky chair beside a table covered with a filthy cloth. 'I read something about it,' he murmured laconically.

'Did yer? O' course, I dunno much, and what I did know I've gorn and forgot. Pity, ain't it?'

'Terrible memory you've got!'

'Yus, Mr. Strange. Shocking.' He waited, and then said heavily: 'Only one thing wot refreshes me old brain-box.'

Jimmy grinned. He brought out a note from his wallet. 'Would this help?'

The other's beery eyes glinted. 'Lumme,

you're a blinking mind-reader!' He smacked his lips. 'It all comes back to me now!'

'You don't say!'

'Nah, Mr. Strange, I did 'ear — ' He bent his mouth close. 'I did 'ear as 'ow the bloke 'ad bin shot and weighted down sos 'e wouldn't swim — so I reckon it must be murder . . . '

'I'm rather under the same impression.'

'Lucky' nodded sagely. 'Queer business. O' course, 'e did know Fenner. And Fenner's a bloke wot wouldn't stop at nothink.'

'Quite.'

Jimmy had strolled over to a window that looked on to the river. He gazed out abstractedly. 'By the way, which is the spot where those schoolboys found Fowler?'

''Bout 'arf a mile down river.'

'Any chance of having a look round there?'

'But, blimey, there ain't nothink there, only water.'

'All the same, I'd like to take a peep.'

'Well, I 'ave got a rowin' boat — not as I want to go lookin' for trouble. Doesn't do when you're in public business.'

Jimmy nodded understandingly.

'No harm in going for a peaceful row.'

'Lucky' scratched his butt head. 'No I suppose not.' He grinned broadly and gave a knowing wink. 'Nice night for a trip, anyway. Come on . . .'

A yellow moon threw a path over the murky river, as a few minutes later 'Lucky', puffing and grunting, wielded the oars in the rusty rowlocks. After some energetic pulling he paused. Mopping his face with a handkerchief, he said:

'About 'ere, it was.'

Jimmy glanced at the ships riding at anchor around them.

'Pretty deep, eh?'

'Deep enough ter drown in,' the other nodded grimly, ' 'specially if you was dead ter start with!' He followed his passenger's gaze to starboard. 'Wot yer lookin' at?'

'The place over there — next to the warehouse. Isn't that Fenner's new gambling joint?'

' 'Sright. The 'Waterfront Club' it's called.'

Jimmy whistled softly. 'Shouldn't be

surprised if it had an exit to the river.'

'I ain't never surprised at nothink,' 'Lucky' grunted.

'Let's go take a look.'

'Orl right.'

They rowed towards the dank, low-lying building adjoining the warehouse. There was a rotting landing stage and some steps leading to a shadowy yard.

'These steps lead to the club, I suppose?' Jimmy said.

' 'Sright.'

'Mightn't be a bad idea if I popped up.'

'Well, pop quiet, then. Don't reckon Fenner welcomes strangers snoopin' round — and the river looks pretty wet tonight.'

Jimmy stepped lightly out of the boat and moved noiselessly across the sagging landing stage.

'I'll wait 'ere,' 'Lucky' called after him in a hoarse whisper. He added: 'Step quiet for heaven's sake!' and dropped an oar with a clatter. 'Blarst the blinkin' oar!'

A soft chuckle came back to him from where Jimmy Strange had melted into the darkness.

'Lucky' held on to a mooring-chain and breathed asthmatically. He sucked at his moustache and watched the dark windows of the 'Waterfront Club'. Mr. Strange seemed to have vanished. He ruminated darkly. Never was such a fellow for popping in and out of the shadows. And he'd turn up from nowhere — just when a bloke was least expecting him. Rum cove! If there was trouble about, he'd always bob up from behind some dark corner. Bit of a mystery. No one knew much about him. If you asked him anything you'd never get no proper answer. He crackled the crisp note in his trousers pocket. Proper gent, though. Always had plenty of money. Wonder what you'd call him. Certainly wasn't a dick. Nor a private 'tec, really. You couldn't call him a crook, neither — though they did say he could crack a crib with the best of 'em. In a good cause. He wasn't a copper's nark . . .

He gave up his speculations. 'A rum cove,' he muttered, 'and that's all you can say about 'im.'

'You can have the rum — I'll take

whisky!' a voice said softly out of the shadows.

'Lucky' almost fell off his seat in surprise. 'Lumme, sir, you didn't 'arf give me a start!' he greeted Jimmy, who was stepping quietly into the boat. 'You been quick.' He grabbed the oars. 'Found out anything?'

'All I want to know.'

' 'Spose it's no good asking you what that is?'

'No harm,' Jimmy chuckled, as he took his place in the stem. 'I just know how to lead Fowler's murderer to his last drop.'

''Strewth!'

Jimmy glanced down at the luminous dial of his wristwatch. 'Put a jerk into it, 'Lucky'!'

'In a hurry?'

'No — but you are. It's nearly closing-time!' And a little later he was sitting in the back parlour of the 'Starboard Light', a large Scotch at his elbow, scribbling a note to Scotland Yard.

★ ★ ★

Scotland Yard next morning.

At a large, handsome mahogany desk, momentous with its documents and dossiers piled on it, sat a sandy-haired, bulky figure with bright-ginger beetling eyebrows and a cleft chin like an inverted wine-bottle. Detective-Inspector Crow's brow was corrugated in great concentration as he bent over a sheaf of papers.

Came a knock on the door.

'Come in!' Crow bellowed, and glared at inoffensive-looking Sergeant Warburton who entered.

'Note for you, sir. Marked 'Urgent'.'

'Urgent, eh? Well, open it and see what it's all about,' he barked. 'I'm busy.' He bent again over his desk.

'Very good, sir.'

'Probably some damned anonymous nonsense,' Crow grumbled.

'No, it's signed all right, sir. Good heavens — well, of all the — '

'What does it say, man?'

'It's written in ink with a pen — '

'Extraordinary!' groaned the long-suffering Inspector with heavy sarcasm. 'Read it.'

'It's only a short note — good-class paper.

'*Read it!*' Crow thumped on the desk. 'Man alive! Can you understand plain English?'

Sergeant Warburton's aesthetic features grew pink. He read the note.

'It says, '*Dear Old Crow*'' — he coughed — ''*I'm sure you'd like to have a cosy chat with a gentleman named Fenner at the 'Waterfront Club' tonight at, say, 10.30. Do pop in: he'd love to see you, and he might tell you something about his old pal Fowler*'.'

Crow sat up with a jerk. He flared explosively. 'Who the hell's that from?' Then he said quickly, 'No, don't tell me!'

'It's signed '*Jimmy Strange*'.'

The Inspector winced. 'Give it me,' he growled. He turned the note over in his hands, muttering to himself: 'Seems to know everything, does our Mr. Strange.'

He pulled a battered pipe from a pocket, lit it thoughtfully. Sergeant Warburton's delicate nostrils wrinkled as the acrid smoke filled the room. 'Waterfront Club' — 10.30,' Crow ruminated.

'I'll need you tonight, Warburton.'

'Very good, sir,' the other coughed.

'Well, don't stand there like that. If you must choke yourself, do it outside!'

The door closed behind Sergeant Warburton while the Inspector continued to glower at the message from Jimmy Strange, puffing in ill-tempered snorts at his foul-smelling pipe.

★　★　★

Promptly at 10.30 that night Detective-Inspector Crow and Sergeant Warburton purposefully entered the 'Waterfront Club'.

Fenner greeted the Inspector with a great show of affability.

'Nice of you to drop in,' he smiled, slapping the other on the shoulder.

'Not at all,' Crow grunted.

He noticed that Fenner's eyes were blood-shot. Been drinking a lot lately, evidently. Held his liquor well, though. An amiable sort of bloke. Outwardly. But not to be trusted. Needed careful handling.

'Always happy to welcome the guardians of the law and all that.'

'I'm sure you are.'

'Absolutely. Any time you — or your Sergeant' — Fenner flashed a smile on Warburton, who remained aloof in the background — 'any time you're passing, always a drink and a cigar for you at the 'Waterfront Club'.'

'Handsome of you.' Crow nodded, peering beneath beetling brows round the office into which Fenner had led them.

'By the way,' the latter was saying in a suitably reverent tone, 'I suppose you've no more news about poor Fowler?'

Crow shot him a penetrating glance. 'Er — no — nothing further,' he muttered. Then added heavily: 'But we hope to have some news pretty soon.'

The other nodded. 'Good. Thought a lot of him, as you can understand. Poor chap! My partner and friend. Anything I can do, only too glad.'

'I'm sure,' the detective grunted non-committally.

He eyed his watch grimly. Ten-thirty-three it registered. His shaggy eyebrows met in a frown. Ten-thirty, Strange had said. Was his letter a trick? A hoax?

Crow's jaw jutted out grimly as the possibility loomed up before him. And yet Strange had never tried that sort of game before.

Fenner was saying: 'I can't imagine *who* could've wanted to murder him.'

'We're wondering the same thing ourselves,' murmured Sergeant Warburton primly. 'Aren't we, sir?'

'Shut up!' retorted Crow.

'Very good, sir.'

The inspector scowled at him. He decided that he'd better take a look round. Matter of routine. Anyway, he couldn't stand there waiting for something to happen. He nodded towards a door facing them.

'Where does that lead to?'

Fenner smiled. 'The river,' he said. 'Down a passage, some steps, a little mooring Jetty, and you're in the drink. Never use it myself. Haven't got a boat.'

Sergeant Warburton was cocking an attentive ear.

'Thought I heard someone out there, sir,' he observed, as the Inspector glared at him.

'Eh?'

Warburton blushed at the other's sceptical grunt.

'Don't think anyone *could* be there,' Fenner said doubtfully.

Even as he spoke his face changed. Footsteps were approaching along the passage. He moved towards the door, his expression one of genuine puzzlement.

'Who the devil — '

'Someone coming up from the river,' Crow said.

The footsteps were outside now. They paused. Fenner halted in his movement to the door. He stood staring at it.

'Anyone there?' he called out suddenly.

No answer. Then the door began to open slowly.

'An unexpected visitor?' Crow had begun to ask heavily, and then broke off with an exclamation.

Framed in the doorway was a figure, grey distorted mask for a face, water dripping from its rotting clothes. A pungent river smell drifted into the room.

Fenner's eyes were popping out of his head as the apparition slowly pointed an emaciated-looking hand at him. Suddenly Fenner gave a horrible, convulsive cry:

'Why, it's *him*!' he croaked. His voice rose hysterically. 'No — no! It can't be! It can't be!'

Crow took a step forward. 'Good lord!' he grunted. 'It's — it's *Fowler*!'

Sergeant Warburton goggled and said, most inelegantly for him: 'Cripes!'

'It isn't!' Fenner's voice cracked. 'It *can't* be Fowler!'

A moaning sound came from the figure in the doorway. Slowly, painfully, it spoke. 'It *is* Fowler . . . Fowler, back from the river . . . '

Fenner flung out an arm as if to ward off the other's advance.

'You couldn't come back!' he babbled. 'You couldn't, I tell you — you're dead!'

The ghastly figure moved slowly towards him. Before its unhurried, implacable approach he backed away. 'You're dead!' His voice became a hoarse whisper. '*I shot you! I shot you!*'

'What!'

It was Crow who turned on him as he cowered, gibbering in terror.

The Inspector moved forward with a grunt of triumph. 'You *did*!'

Fenner seemed oblivious of the presence of the Scotland Yard man.

Oblivious even of his self-admitted guilt, his whole attention was fixed in terrified concentration upon the thing in front of him. It was speaking again:

'You murdered me . . . so you thought . . . but I have come back!'

Fenner was in a state bordering on collapse as the Inspector closed with him purposefully, nodding to Sergeant Warburton to aid him. The Sergeant was gaping at the apparition as if transfixed.

'Come on,' rasped Crow, 'don't stand there like a bar of soap! Take charge of him!'

Warburton snapped out of his trance sufficiently to move to Fenner's side and grasp his arm. The action was necessary more as a means of support than to bar his escape. The man was shaking with terror and babbling as if in a delirium. Observing this with satisfaction, and convinced that there was no chance of his attempting a getaway, the more solid

Inspector Crow turned to give his attention to the eerie visitor who had been so effectively responsible for Fenner's dramatic revelation. Now it was his turn to gape.

The apparition had vanished.

'Well, I'll be damned!' he growled.

The door through which the figure had appeared was still open, and he thought he detected the sound of footsteps retreating quickly down the passage towards the river. He was about to hurry forward to investigate when the door handle behind him turned. He wheeled round with a scowl. 'Who the — ' he began, and then his ginger eyebrows drew closer, even more aggressively. His jaw clamped together like a rat-trap as he glowered at the newcomer.

It was Jimmy Strange who lounged casually in the doorway.

'Good evening,' he grinned easily. 'Thought I'd look in to ask you to have a drink before you go. Got one waiting for you at the bar . . . '

He blew a cloud of smoke from his cigarette. The smile still quirked the corners of his mouth while his gaze wandered over to where Sergeant Warburton, half supporting a white, nerve-shattered Fenner stared at him with prim disapproval. Jimmy gave him a wink, then glanced at the door of the passage. Without a change of expression he turned to the Inspector and said lightly:

'What's the matter, Crow. Old bird? Better come and have that drink!' He added, 'You look as if you'd seen a ghost.'

★   ★   ★

Jimmy Strange was in company with a number of others, propping up the bar of 'Joe's Place' in Greek Street. It was the following evening. Perched on a stool next to him, soft hat on the back of his head, a good-looking young man was saying:

'And when Dad threatened to squeal about the crooked way Fenner was running the club, he was just put out of the way?'

Jimmy nodded. He finished his drink. He indicated the other's empty glass and said, 'Could you use another?'

'Could a duck swim?' young Fowler said.

Jimmy gave the order and lit a cigarette. The barman came back with the drinks, and he took his and said:

'Well, here's to the greatest performance of your career.'

The other grinned, made an elaborate bow. 'Thank you. Pity one or two London producers weren't there to see it!'

Jimmy nodded sympathetically. 'Pity. Still, old Crow liked it.' He paused thoughtfully, then mused: 'Yes . . . you must have put up a pretty convincing show to have frightened the wits out of Fenner the way you did!'

He turned the idea over in his mind with evident satisfaction and grinned at the other over the rim of his glass. Then:

'Cheerio,' said Jimmy Strange, and added, 'then I must be hopping it. Got another bar waiting for me to lean against.'

He paused suddenly as he was about to drink, murmuring half to himself:

'And this time I really mustn't keep her waiting.'

4

The Lady with the Gun

It was 6.30 in the evening when Sandra 'phoned.

'You're going to be absolutely livid with me — '

'What makes you imagine that?'

Jimmy's smile as he interrupted her was tinged with not a little sardonic amusement. There was the suspicion of an edge to his voice. In other words, he had a feeling he knew what was coming. He went on:

'Could it be, for instance, you're about to tell me you can't make it tonight?'

'Well — yes — darling. You see — '

But again he cut in. 'Having left it so late,' he said remorselessly, 'so I can't take a little red-headed number I know instead.'

She said:

'You're a beast, and I hate you.' Jimmy

chuckled into the 'phone, and she continued: 'I *did* feel awfully upset letting you down at the last minute — '

'Thank you for that, darling — '

'But now I don't give a damn. And I'm sure, with that irresistible charm of yours, you'll find some other piece just as attractive as your redhead who'll be crazy to go to the theatre with you.'

The bite behind her words was sharp enough to cut through steel, he reflected. He said:

'I'll certainly run through my list and see what I can do.'

'In fact,' she went on, 'you'll no doubt have a simply wonderful evening, and in the end be glad I couldn't make it.'

'You read me like a book,' he chuckled.

'One of the flashy-covered kind they keep under the counter in dirty back-street shops.'

'You *do* get around.' And chuckled again as he heard her 'Oh!' of exasperation. 'I suppose,' he said, 'the reason you can't come along is because your aunt's turned up unexpectedly from the country?'

'Very witty,' she said.

'You tell me,' he encouraged her.

'I really don't see why I should. And, anyway,' she added icily, 'wouldn't you rather I rang off so you can call one of your many girlfriends who're languishing by their 'phones just in the hope you may ring them?'

'All right, Sandra,' he said evenly. 'Cut the comedy and come to earth. Tell Jimmy, what's on your mind and let's fix a date for tomorrow.'

'You won't take another woman tonight?'

Her voice came over the wire now soft and huskily appealing. The old black magic she was putting on. But that was the way he liked it. He said:

'Sweetness, you know me. Just a one-woman man.'

'Liar!'

But she was laughing, and she went on: 'Oh, Jimmy, I *am* sorry about this evening, honest. But — '

'I know, these aunts can be a bore,' he said helpfully.

'Shut up! I haven't got an aunt. It's my sister.'

'Sister?' he cut in quickly. A trifle too quickly, maybe.

'Take it easy, my pet. She's already signed up by a really nice man. They're getting married soon.' And added — for his especial benefit, he decided: 'It's a thing people do sometimes.'

He said at once:

'So do people jump off cliffs.'

'I suppose you think that's amusing?'

'You were saying about your sister,' he reminded her.

'She's in town unexpectedly, just for tonight. I haven't seen her since I've been here and so — well, I've promised her I'd have food with her. You do understand, darling?'

'Sure,' he said easily. 'Go along and have a good time.'

'You'll 'phone me in the morning?'

'I'll do that very little thing,' he said.

And after she'd reiterated how sorry she was, and he'd said it would give him a chance to spend a quiet evening for a change — a remark she frankly disbelieved and said so — Jimmy hung up.

From which it may be gathered that

Jimmy Strange had not lost his grip of the Sandra situation. Far from it. In fact, it was progressing pretty much along the lines he thought he would like it to go. This in spite of his outrageously nonchalant behaviour at the 'Mirrobar' the night of the Fenner episode. When he'd left her almost breathless with bewilderment and she'd had to go home all on her ownsome. True, he'd fixed the taxi for her, but a taxi with no one to share it with isn't rated much of a consolation by a pretty girl.

With anyone else, of course, that would have been that. Definitely. But he wasn't anyone else. He grew on her, and what in anyone else would have appeared impossible in him had an intriguing angle. She came back for more.

Women, as has been recorded on occasion, being funny that way.

All this was fine with Jimmy too. As far as it went. There lay the tiniest suggestion, the mere hint, of a snag that might trip him, and in the not-too-distant future. If he didn't keep his eyes peeled. For he held the uneasy suspicion that

Sandra wouldn't object to marrying him. Wouldn't object at all. Which was going too far. Much too far. Definitely.

The trouble was she was so attractive. And there might come a moment when he might lose his head to the extent of waking up one morning with the sound of wedding-bells in his ears and the scent of orange-blossom all around.

Jimmy shuddered at the idea and went out for a drink.

Which was why some time later he was to be found indulging in his not-unfamiliar pastime of helping prop up the bar of 'Joe's Place' in Greek Street. While he was putting his hand in his inside pocket for his wallet to pay for a liberal libation that had just been placed before him he found two theatre tickets. He considered them idly. They had been given him by a theatre-manager friend of young Fisher as it happened, and were for the show to which he had been taking Sandra. The curtain was due to go up in twenty minutes. He shrugged, he was at a loose end, but had no inclination for playgoing alone.

Then he had a sudden quixotic thought. He would stroll along towards the theatre and the first person he met whom he knew he'd ask to accompany him to the play. It seemed a pity that two seats for what he'd heard was a good show should go begging. If he didn't meet anyone of his acquaintance, then he'd turn the idea in, have a couple of drinks and go home.

As it happened, he was destined not to have an early night, for as he turned into Shaftesbury Avenue he ran into Dr. Michael Vance.

'Jimmy Strange! Well, well, just imagine.'

'Hello there, Mike.'

He'd known the doctor for several years — at one time they'd lived next door to each other in the same block of flats. Vance was saying he'd just dined at a nearby restaurant after an arduous day's work and was now homeward bound intending to put in a few hours' study before retiring to bed. By his tone he evidently didn't relish the prospect, and Jimmy pounced on him.

'Take a night off for once,' he urged him. 'Come to the theatre with me. I've a couple of seats for 'The Mask' doing nothing.'

The other looked at him quizzically. 'What's likely to happen there? A robbery, a murder, or just plain mayhem?'

Jimmy grinned. 'Nothing's going to happen except what's supposed to on the stage.'

Vance eyed him doubtfully. 'When Jimmy Strange puts in a personal appearance, I should've thought there'd be much more lurid drama enacted in the *stalls*!'

Jimmy smiled again. He said, 'I didn't know my reputation had got around to Harley Street!' He finally persuaded Vance, whom he was pleased to see again, into putting aside any further thoughts of work for the night, and together they went along to 'The Mask'. The play was a melodrama calculated to have the most *blasé* hanging on to his seat with excitement. The doctor was appropriately thrilled, and even Jimmy, though not unaccustomed to dramatic highlights in real life, was good-humouredly enjoying a busman's holiday.

It was just before the curtain of the second act. The 'big' scene of the play was building up to its climax. The two stars of the show, Gloria Allen and Charles Russell, were on the stage alone. The latter, in the role of charming and worldly-wise philanderer, was attempting to placate the woman who had suddenly arrived at his flat demanding a show-down. The woman had pulled a revolver from her handbag. The audience was tense with suppressed excitement as the man grovelled at her feet imploring her not to shoot.

Jimmy noted with interest the expert way the actress handled the gun. She slipped back the safety-catch in a style that was firmly businesslike as she levelled it at the man. She held the gun as though she really knew how. Came the moment of peak tension. Grimly she took a step forward and pressed the trigger. There was a realistic report. The actor groaned and sagged, his face contorted agoniz-ingly. First-rate stuff, Jimmy conceded, as the curtain came down to tumultuous applause.

'Damned good, eh, old man?' Vance was saying, applauding with enthusiasm.

'Not bad. Not bad at all.'

'Oh, you're so hardboiled!'

'Maybe . . . let's go and find the bar.'

'Good idea,' the other agreed, then exclaimed: 'Hello, what's happening?'

Jimmy watched a plump individual, somewhat resembling a rather harassed penguin in his white tie and tails, hold up his hand as he stepped through the curtains to the footlights.

'Ladies and gentlemen, if there is a doctor present, would he please come round immediately? There — there's been an accident.'

As the speculative hum of chatter arose around them, Jimmy grinned at his companion.

'Looks as if you'll have to do some work tonight after all!'

Vance nodded, and raised a hand to attract the attention of the man on the stage.

'Oh, thank you,' was the fervent

response across the footlights. 'If you'd just step through the pass-door at the side . . . '

Vance said to Jimmy: 'Coming with me?'

'I'd sooner go and have that drink.'

'It may be interesting.'

'As interesting as a large Scotch?'

'You can have that later,' the other promised him.

'All right. I'm with you.'

The man in the white tie and tails greeted them as they pushed through a narrow door at the head of a short flight of stairs opening on to the stage. He introduced himself as the manager of the theatre.

'A very serious accident, I'm afraid,' he said in answer to the doctor's question. 'Charles Russell has been shot. He's in his dressing room — if you'd come this way.' They followed him across the stage, past spot-lamps and scenery, and down a passage.

'Here. This room.' The manager pushed open a door. Jimmy took one look at the body of Charles Russell, which lay on a couch, then glanced sharply at Gloria Allen, who turned and faced them as they came in. She was weeping, the tears running down her face, grotesquely smearing her stage make-up,

'It's terrible!' she moaned hysterically. 'Terrible!'

Vance bent quickly over the inert figure on the couch. After a brief examination he looked up, his face grave.

'He's dead, I'm afraid. Bullet entered the heart. Must have been instantaneous,'

The actress moved across and grasped his arm. 'Can't you do something?' she begged. 'He *can't* be dead! He *can't* be!'

The doctor shook his head gently. 'There's nothing we can do.'

'Charles! Oh, poor Charles!'

The manager slipped an arm round her shoulders. 'Now, my dear, you must try and calm yourself — '

She broke into uncontrollable sobs and flung herself into a chair.

'Please, Miss Allen, you must pull yourself together.' The other gazed at her helplessly. Then he turned to Jimmy and Vance. 'I — er — I must tell the audience,' he said unsteadily. 'We can't go on, that's certain.' He looked at the doctor. 'I suppose one ought to send for the police?'

'Certainly.'

Gloria Allen jerked up her blonde head. Fear seemed to have replaced her grief for the moment.

'They won't think *I* did it?' she said in a low voice. 'They won't arrest me?'

'No, of course not,' the manager reassured her quickly. 'You've nothing to fear — it was an accident . . . Now, wouldn't you like to go back to your dressing room?'

She rose unsteadily to her feet, clutching the back of the chair.

'Poor Charles!' she moaned. 'I can't believe it's happened.'

Jimmy stepped forward and took her arm. 'Let me take you to your room. I'll get you a drink. You'll feel better.'

And a few minutes later, having procured a drink for her plus a large one for himself, he was sitting in the actress's dressing room listening to her account of the tragedy. She seemed much more calm now. She was saying:

'You see, the revolver is always brought to me just before the second act starts.'

He nodded and tapped the ash off his cigarette.

'Where d'you put it when you go on the stage at the beginning of the act?'

'I leave it here on my dressing-table ready for the quick change I have just before the shooting scene.'

'And that's when you take the gun?'

'Yes.'

'I see.' He considered her for a moment through a puff of cigarette smoke. Then: 'While it's left on the table, could anyone pop in and — er — fiddle with it?'

'Oh no, my dresser's here all the time.'

'Sure?'

'Perfectly sure. Oh, I — ' She broke off as though she'd suddenly remembered something.

'What?'

'I forgot. She goes down on the stage for a few minutes — '

'When?'

'Just before my change.'

'How long is the room empty?'

'Five minutes at the most.'

Jimmy took a gulp from his glass and his gaze wandered round the dressing room. He crossed over to a window across which curtains were drawn. He pulled one aside. The window was slightly open. 'Where does this lead to?'

'The fire-escape.' Suddenly she was looking at him through narrowed eyes. She stood up aggressively, saying: 'You're asking a lot of questions. Are you a reporter?'

'Good lord, no!'

'A detective, then?'

He smiled at her disarmingly. 'Have you noticed my policeman's boots? No,' he said easily, moving over to her. 'I just happen to be a friend of Dr. Vance. I'm trying to be — er — helpful, that's all.'

There was a knock on the door, and a grizzled little man put his head into the room.

'Oh, Miss Allen, it's Mr. Russell's cousin at the stage door — '

She gave a little gasp. Twisted her hands together in agitation. 'Have you — have you told him . . . ?'

'About the accident, miss? No, I didn't like to.'

She hesitated a moment, then drew a deep breath.

'You'd better ask him to come and see me then. I'll tell him.'

The stage-door keeper shifted from one foot to the other and mumbled:

''Fraid I can't let 'im along to your dressing room. Yer see — '

'Why not?'

'It's the perlice — '

Her hands flew to her throat.

'They've arrived?' The words were a whisper.

'And they said I wasn't ter let no one out nor in.'

Jimmy moved over to her and said, 'How would it be if I told him what's happened?'

'Would you?' She gave him a tremulous look of gratitude,

'Leave it to me.' At the door he turned. 'By the way, what's his name?'

'Paul Carfax.'

'I'll take you to him.' the little man said, and led the way. Carfax was leaning against the stage-door keeper's cubby-hole, impatiently tapping his silver-mounted walking stick.

Jimmy noted he was tall, debonair, in impeccable evening dress and opera hat.

'What's all the trouble?' he greeted Jimmy irritably. 'I never have this fuss as a rule when I want to come in — '

'I'm afraid your cousin's met with an accident.'

'Charles? Good heavens!' He almost dropped his walking stick. 'Nothing serious?'

Jimmy eyed him. He said: 'Very serious. He's dead.'

'Dead? But — but — ' Carfax goggled at him unbelievingly. 'But this is awful! How — when did it happen? Is Mrs. Russell here?' His words ran into each other.

'His wife?' Jimmy said.

The other nodded.

'I'm not sure that she's been told.'

'She ought to know.' Carfax appeared to pull himself together. 'I'd — I'd better ring her at once.'

'There's a telephone in 'ere,' offered

the stage-door keeper from his cubbyhole.

Hurriedly Carfax rang a number.

'Hello . . . It's Mr. Carfax. I want to speak to Mrs. Russell — wait a moment. Has anyone 'phoned from the theatre? No? Well, hurry and find her, will you?'

While he was waiting, he glanced round and saw Jimmy grinding a cigarette-stub under his heel.

'What a terrible business!' he muttered. 'I was always warning Charles about that gun, you know — ' He broke off and spoke into the mouthpiece again. 'That you, Margaret? Paul here. Can I come round and see you . . . ? Yes, straight away. Right. Goodbye.' He hung up and rejoined Jimmy.

'Poor woman! How the hell am I going to break it to her? She was devoted to him.' He turned to the stage-door keeper. 'Look here, I can't tell Mrs. Russell what's happened without having seen her husband first — '

'No one ain't to come in nor go out — police orders.'

Carfax stared at him. 'The police are here?'

122

The other nodded. Carfax swallowed and glanced at Jimmy, who said, 'I think it would be all right for Mr. Carfax to go to the dressing room — he *is* a relative.'

The grizzled little man shrugged his shoulders and grumbled non-committally, 'I can't stop no one by force. I'm just repeating me orders.'

Carfax said, 'I'll speak to the police first, and explain who I am — I'm sure they'll let me see him and then break the news to Mrs. Russell.'

Jimmy nodded. 'You go ahead.'

After he'd disappeared along the passage, Jimmy peered into the cubby-hole.

'Lorst anythink, sir?'

'I'm looking for the 'phone-book.'

The other dived down out of sight with a rheumatic grunt. His voice rose up from the floor. 'I keeps 'em down 'ere to put me feet on so's I won't catch cold on this 'ere stone floor.' More grunting. 'Which'll you 'ave, sir — A to K or L to Z?'

'A to K.'

The book appeared as if from nowhere, and Jimmy quickly flipped the pages. The stage-door keeper rose into view, wheezing like some old walrus and watched him. He said conversationally: 'Perlice started asking me questions. Not that I could tell 'em much. Blimey, but 'e don't 'arf snap yer 'ead orf that deteckertive don't!'

'Does he?'

'Ar. Bad-tempered bloke. Read 'is name in the papers, I 'ave — Inspector Hawk, or Jay, or some such name — '

Jimmy's head jerked up.

'What! My old friend Inspector Crow?'

'That's 'im. Pal o' yours?'

Jimmy chuckled. 'Yes and no.' He sighed. 'Ah well, it's a small world.' Then to himself he murmured: 'Fancy the old Crow being on the job. I shall have to get a move on.' He handed the directory back to the other.

'Find wot yer wanted, sir?'

Jimmy nodded. Exaggeratedly he licked his lips, 'My, my, I've got a thirst I wouldn't sell for a million! I'll just pop out for a quick one.'

'No one ain't supposed to leave . . . ' the stage-door keeper began, then saw the note Jimmy slid across to him. 'Oh well, sir, make it snappy, won't yer?'

Jimmy Strange had vanished. A moment later he was turning the corner of the narrow street running behind the theatre when he stopped suddenly. Approaching him came the tap-tap of a walking stick on the pavement, and a whining voice intoning monotonously.

'Spare a copper for the blind. Copper for the blind, please.'

Jimmy grinned to himself, and waited as a seedy-looking individual approached, His eyes were hidden by dark glasses and he shuffled his way haltingly, tapping his white-painted stick in front of him. Slung round his neck was a chipped enamel cup and a dirty piece of cardboard with the word 'Blind' scrawled across it.

'Hello, Eddie,' Jimmy greeted him.

' 'Ello, Mr. Strange.'

'Still up to your tricks?'

'Not so loud,' the man whined under his breath. 'Yer'll get me inter trouble.'

'Can you use a drink?'

'Don't mind if I do.' He tapped his way to the kerb and muttered from the side of his mouth: 'Lead me across the road, will yer? Looks bad else.'

A few minutes later Eddie was raising his glass and saying:

''Ere's 'ow, guv'nor!'

'Good luck.'

Eddie took a long gulp, then smacked his lips noisily.

'Ah! Bit of orl right, that is.' Then he added with a studied casualness: 'Bin some goings-on over at *The Mask*, ain't there?'

Jimmy raised an eyebrow.

'What d'you know about it?'

'Quite a bit.' And he drained his glass.

'Same again,' Jimmy called to the barman, and said to the other: 'Tell me more.'

'Only that I seen the thief on the job, I did.'

'Thief?'

Eddie took the pint that was placed before him, eyed it with a connoisseur's gaze, nodded appreciatively, and said: 'I 'appens ter be in the alley back o' the theatre — '

'So?'

'I often goes there for a bite o' supper afore I starts workin' the audiences comin' out,' Eddie explained, 'and ter-night I sees this bloke nip up the fire escape and 'op through a winder.'

'What time was this?'

'Somewhere about quarter past nine it 'ud be.'

Jimmy nodded. 'Very interesting.'

'Tallish chap 'e looked. In a dark coat and 'at like 'e might've bin in evenin' dress.'

'Very interesting indeed.'

The other cocked his dark glasses up at him. 'One of them jool thieves, p'raps, eh?' he speculated.

'Perhaps.' Jimmy finished his whisky. 'Well, I must be popping along — '

'S'long, guv'nor.' He caught Jimmy's sleeve. ' 'Ere, yer won't say nothing about wot I saw, will yer? Ruin me business if yer did.'

Jimmy chuckled. 'I'd hate to do that, Eddie.'

In the street he got a taxi.

'Carlton Mansions, Duke Street. Hurry!'

The taxi drew up at the entrance to a

modern block of flats. Jimmy went in and unhurriedly took himself up in the self-operating lift to the fourth floor. He located Paul Carfax's flat and, keeping a watchful eye about him, he bent before the patent lock.

A few minutes' concentrated and deft manipulation, and he stood inside the flat, the door closed behind him. It was a two-roomed place. Bedroom, sitting room, bathroom and kitchenette. The sitting room occupied Jimmy's attention first. He drew the curtains, clicked on the light and began his search. As he was shutting the drawer of a Louis Quinze desk he suddenly stood upright, listening.

Unmistakably he caught the scrape of a key in the lock of the flat door. He glanced around him, tensed, and eyes narrowed. No chance of getting out through the flat door now unless the visitor made for the bathroom or the bedroom first. He wouldn't risk taking that chance.

With a swift movement he snapped off the light, and found his way behind the long curtains that covered the window. He suddenly realized that there was a gap of six inches between the bottom of the curtain and the floor. Quickly he placed his hands on the window-ledge behind him and hoisted himself up so that his feet were out of sight.

The door was being opened. The light came on. Footsteps approached across the thick carpet, and a whiff of perfume told Jimmy the visitor was a woman.

His wrists ached with bracing himself by the window frame, perspiration began to bead his forehead, but he set his teeth and kept himself suspended from the newcomer's view. He heard her lift the telephone receiver and dial.

'Mrs. Russell speaking . . . Oh, Marie, I'm expecting Mr. Carfax to call. When he comes, tell him I've gone on to his flat. I'll wait for him here.'

It was a clipped, brittle voice belonging to a woman of about thirty-five, as far as Jimmy could judge. She rang off. He heard her moving about the room.

So Charles Russell's wife had a key to Paul Carfax's flat, had she! Hmm . . .

things were growing more and more interesting . . . If only his wrists didn't seem on fire. Damn! Wasn't she ever going? She was opening and shutting drawers now. There was the rustle of paper. She was on the right-hand side of the room, and Jimmy, through a corner of the curtains, caught a brief glimpse of her. Handsome, raven-haired type she was. Then she had disappeared out of sight. It was eerie not knowing where she was in the room. Her footsteps were noiseless over the thick carpet and gave little indication of where she was exactly.

He was becoming increasingly conscious of the cramp in his arms. The strain on his wrists was intolerable. It was no good, he couldn't hang on any longer. He lowered himself to the floor.

He tensed himself as he heard the quick intake of the woman's breath. Then came the rasp of a drawer being opened. Suddenly a jewelled hand grasped the curtain and pulled it aside.

Jimmy found himself staring into the cold-quartz eyes of Mrs. Russell. He grinned at her nonchalantly rubbed his wrists and his eyes travelled to the small but business-like automatic that she pointed at him.

'What are you doing here?'

Jimmy's smile was most engaging. 'As a matter of fact, I'm waiting for Paul — er — Mr. Carfax, you know. He's a friend of mine.'

'Then why were you hiding behind the curtains?'

'I'm afraid it's rather a long story.' He shrugged. 'Might bore you — '

'It won't,' she snapped grimly. 'Go on.'

'Well — I — er — I thought I heard a fire engine bell. Now fire engines have always had a strange fascination for me. I went to the window to look out, leaned on the ledge, and then — er — then — '

'Well?'

'I — er — I suppose I must have dozed off.'

Her lips twisted contemptuously. 'You're lying, of course.'

He returned her look with one of pained innocence. She said:

'How did you get into the flat?'

'The door was open. Paul said it would be.'

'Nonsense! He never leaves the door open. He's too careful — ' She broke off.

'Careful of what?' Jimmy pursued gently. 'Has he anything to hide?'

'How dare you question me!' Her eyes blazed.

'Perhaps he'd hidden something you wanted to find?' he queried, his gaze blandly ingenuous. 'After all, a woman doesn't normally search her — er — boyfriend's flat.' He smiled charmingly. 'Not if she's a nice woman — and he's a nice boyfriend!'

'You — !' She gripped the gun so that her knuckles were white. 'Stay where you are! I'm going to 'phone the police.'

'Go ahead.'

She backed to the telephone, keeping the automatic levelled at him menacingly. She lifted the receiver, paused thoughtfully and replaced it.

Jimmy grinned. He said easily, 'Changed your mind, Mrs. Russell?'

She moved towards him, still with the gun threatening him.

'Paul will be here soon. He'll deal with you. I warn you — he's a very impatient man.'

'So I understand.'

'Stand where you are. Don't move an inch!'

Jimmy advanced towards her calmly.

'Interesting little gun you have, Mrs. Russell. Firearms fascinate me almost as much as fire engines. May I see it?'

'I warn you — '

Suddenly Jimmy pounced forward and shot out his hand, knocking her arm up sharply. She was so surprised by the swiftness of his movement that she didn't press the trigger. In a flash he closed with her, grabbing her wrist and giving it a deft twist. The gun spun from her grasp; as she made an effort to retrieve it, Jimmy quickly picked it up with his free hand. He released her and she drew back her hand to her throat. He stood between her and the door.

'What — what are you going to do?' she gasped.

Holding the automatic with elaborate casualness, he extracted his cigarette case,

133

lit a cigarette and smiled at her through a cloud of tobacco smoke.

'If you dare to touch me I'll scream!'

Jimmy laughed shortly. 'You flatter yourself, my dear Mrs. Russell. Frankly, you're *not* my type!'

'You beast!'

'Oh, never mind,' he commiserated. 'I dare say you're the cream in Carfax's coffee all right. Step smartly backwards — through the door — that's the idea.'

'Where are you taking me?'

'I'm not taking you anywhere. Just leaving you — in time to cool yourself down, and think up a story ready for the police when they arrive.'

Her face livid, she backed down the passage to where the bathroom door stood slightly open.

'Switch on the light,' he ordered her.

She put a hand behind her, felt for the switch and snapped it on. He urged her backwards into the bathroom with a movement of his gun, gave a quick glance round that satisfied him there was no means of escape for her, then, removing the key to the outside of the lock, slammed the door and locked it.

With a grim smile he returned quickly to the sitting room. With expert swiftness he turned out drawers and cupboards. He did not bother to cover up his searching. There was no time for that. He did not want to be interrupted again. Quickly he worked, oblivious of Mrs. Russell, who was beating on the bathroom door and hurling a stream of abuse at him that revealed her to be only superficially a lady.

'Shocking! Quite shocking!' Jimmy murmured to himself. Then he paused to survey the drawer he was turning out with narrowed eyes. 'Hello! What's this?'

He picked out three small boxes. Two of them were of the dark blue velvet-lined type used by jewellers. The third was a soiled plain cardboard box secured by an elastic band. He opened the blue receptacles, saw that one contained a gold dress-watch and the other a pair of platinum and onyx cufflinks.

With a little sigh he returned these to the drawer. The other cardboard box he put in his pocket. From its contents he knew this was what Mrs. Russell had been seeking so desperately — evidence that she wanted hidden from the police.

Quietly Jimmy slipped out of the flat, closing the door behind him. The muffled cries of the incarcerated Mrs. Russell followed him to the lift.

He took a taxi from the rank in Duke Street.

"'Mask' Theatre — quick as you can!'

*   *   *

On the brightly lit stage of the 'Mask' Theatre, Gloria Allen was re-enacting the scene at the end of the second act in which she had fired the shot that had killed Charles Russell. Sergeant Warburton stood behind the Inspector, eying the proceedings with prim disapproval, as if he thought that this play-acting business had caused enough trouble as it was, without going through the business again. From the wings the manager and Dr. Vance watched attentively.

'Very well, Miss Allen,' Inspector Crow

grunted. 'I think that'll be all for the moment.'

'That's exactly how it happened.' She turned to him appealingly. 'And I had no more idea that the revolver was *really* loaded than — '

The detective cut her short impatiently.

'I know. You told me.' His beetle brows met in a sandy line of cogitation. He turned to Sergeant Warburton.

'I'd like another word with the property-man about the revolver.'

'The property-man, sir?' the Sergeant queried somewhat absently.

'Yes — don't stand there day-dreaming. Find him!'

'Very good, sir,' the Sergeant murmured.

'And don't take all night. Put a jerk into it!'

Sergeant Warburton blushed beneath his superior's rising irascibility, but made no move. Instead he held up a finger, one ear cocked intently.

'Excuse me, Inspector,' he coughed apologetically. 'I think I hear music.' His eyes went dreamy. 'Yes, indeed, sir.

Definitely. Something from one of the Italian operas, I imagine. Quite haunting, sir.'

'Music!' spluttered the Inspector, moving forward with a roar. 'I'll haunt you if you don't — '

The manager suddenly interrupted. 'He's right, I can hear it now. It's someone whistling.' He stepped quickly on to the stage, his face puzzled. 'There must be someone in the auditorium.'

'The devil there is!' Inspector Crow growled, and listened as unmistakably there came from somewhere on the other side of the curtain the sound of someone whistling the melody from the overture to *Pagliácci*.

He barked, 'Get the curtain up!'

'Why, certainly, Inspector.' The manager shouted up into the dark tangle of ropes and suspended scenery above their heads.

'I say, there, somebody take up that curtain!'

A voice came down with Cockney alacrity. 'Right-o, sir. Goin' up nah.'

'Hurry, man,' grumbled Crow. 'Hurry!'

'Okay, chief!' chirped the voice again.

The curtain rose. The manager pointed excitedly.

'Look! Somebody in the balcony!'

As the light released by the curtain flooded the front of the auditorium, Jimmy Strange stepped back into the shadows of the balcony.

He had stopped whistling. He called down to the group gaping up at him.

'Hello, Crow.'

'Strange! What the hell are you doing up there?'

'Oh, just watching the show! You know — on with the motley the paint and the powder and what-have-you — '

The Inspector choked apoplectically. Then he found his voice and bawled: 'Come down!'

'I'm quite cosy here, thanks. Some other time — perhaps!'

Crow spluttered. With a tremendous effort he contrived to calm himself. He gritted his teeth and said grimly: 'Perhaps you don't realize we've some very serious business on here? A man's died.'

'I know,' replied Jimmy elaborately

stifling a yawn. 'I also know who killed him.'

There were gasps and murmurs from the little group on the stage.

Crow goggled, then lumbered to the footlights, his heavy bottle-shaped haw sticking out.

'*What* are you saying?'

'My, my! You *do* look dramatic,' Jimmy chuckled. 'Just like a scene from a detective play!' He stepped out of the shadows for a moment holding up the cardboard box he had found in Carfax's flat.

'Well, here's a clue for you to be going on with — catch!'

'What the blazes —' Inspector Crow broke off as the cardboard box flew towards the stage.

'All right, sir, I've caught it!' Sergeant Warburton said, in tones of mixed surprise and pride. 'Fancy that! And me no good at cricket!'

'Give it to me!' Crow bellowed, and grabbed the box.

'Be careful how you open it,' called Jimmy warningly. 'There'll be fingerprints.'

The Inspector was ripping off the elastic band.

'A packet of cartridges!' he gasped.

Jimmy said: 'As you see, Crow, old bird, there's one missing — which I think you'll find is the one that killed Russell.'

'Good heavens!' said the manager, and the others moved forward towards the Inspector, staring at the box.

'Well, I never!' said Sergeant Warburton, his eyes popping. 'There *is* one missing and all!'

'Hell!' said Crow. 'Where did you get this, Strange?'

'Paul Carfax's flat in Duke Street.' Jimmy moved farther back into the darkness until only the tip of his cigarette showed plainly. As he made for the balcony exit, he called over his shoulder 'If you hurry, you'll find him breaking down the door of his own bathroom. He chuckled. 'Mrs. Russell's inside!'

And with the *Pagliácci* melody on his lips he was gone.

★　★　★

Some time later Dr. Vance was saying in suitably admiring tones over a drink: 'Why did Paul Carfax do it, Jimmy?'

'He was in love with Russell's wife. Russell wouldn't give her a divorce. He was also heavily insured I should imagine. That infernal triangle again.'

'How did you *know* he did it? You were taking a long shot, weren't you?'

Jimmy grinned easily. 'Carfax slipped up when he told me at the stage door he'd always warned Russell about the gun. Yet no one had told him his cousin was shot. Rather careless of him, wasn't it?'

And, lighting a cigarette, he called to the barman:

'Some more of that medicine the doctor ordered. It's a real cure.'

5

The Queer Fish

'At the risk of sounding old-fashioned, I've come to the conclusion a girl shouldn't let herself be made love to — except by the man she's going to marry.'

Sandra gave Jimmy a sidelong glance from beneath her heavy eyelashes and carried on with the repair work on her make-up. Despite the jolting of the taxi which bore them through the narrow streets of London's Dockland she manipulated her lipstick deftly.

Jimmy, who'd been responsible for the damage she was renovating, regarded her with a raised eyebrow. He hadn't noticed that the resistance she'd put up against his advances had been altogether insurmountable.

He said: 'Why this sudden change of mood?'

'Isn't fair to my husband,' she said.

He stared at her. 'But you haven't got a husband — or would this be something you've been holding out on me?'

She said: 'I shall have a husband sooner or later,' and gave him a look.

He decided the glint in her lovely eyes was of a dangerously speculative nature. He coughed and lit a cigarette.

She went on: 'And he might be jealous.' She put a hand on his arm. 'Don't think I don't like you, darling. I do. Or that I've forgotten what you did for Philip — '

He cut her short. 'Forget it.'

Her smile was tender.

'Trouble is I'm growing fond of you, Jimmy. And a girl doesn't want to get too fond of — '

'Of a guy like me?'

'Well . . . you wouldn't describe yourself as the marrying type exactly. Or would you?'

He grinned at her amiably. His answer she knew lay in that disarming smile that caught at her heart. She gave a little sigh, then said brightly, 'Cigarette?'

He lit one for her.

They'd been seeing her brother off

from Tilbury. After the ship bearing him to South Africa had slid down-river into the gathering dusk, Jimmy had suggested a place to drink a bon voyage to Philip — this being as good excuse as any he could think up for the double Scotch he was in need of. And so the taxi was bound for the 'Queer Fish', that picturesque little dockside pub and caravanserai for all travellers of the seven seas. They were drawing up outside it now.

Jimmy led the way, pushing through the swing-doors.

A babel of voices and clink of glasses greeted them. Tobacco smoke and the fumes of liquor stung Sandra's eyes. Jimmy indicated the walls crowded with curios and souvenirs bartered for refreshment by customers over many thirsty years.

'Comic-looking place, eh?'

Sandra was eyeing a swarthy-looking character lounging near the door. He had a scar that ran from ear to mouth.

'I — I don't know that it's at all funny!' she said, with some apprehension.

'Mustn't judge by appearances. It's a good spot really.'

'You've been here often?'

'Now and again. The owner's a pal of mine. You'll like him. Nice chap — even though some of his customers are rather odd.'

'Let's sit in this corner and hope for the best, anyway.'

'He keeps a good brand of whisky.'

'So that's the attraction?' She smiled up at him.

'He's got a pretty daughter, too, 'matter of fact.'

'Nice for him!'

'And for the customers,' he said. 'Though personally I fall for the whisky! What'll you drink?'

'A dry sherry, please.'

'Park here while I just say hello to Cicero and bring the poison.'

'Who's Cicero?'

'Bloke who owns the place — that's him behind the bar.'

'The fat man?'

'Yes.'

'Cicero,' she echoed. 'What a marvellous name.'

'He's a marvellous chap. Used to be a

146

sea-captain. Been all over the world and all that.'

'I wonder why he was called Cicero?' she puzzled.

'He says his mother christened him that way because she wanted a girl and she thought it was a girl's name. I won't be a minute.'

He went over to the bar where a large fat man was swilling glasses.

'Hello there!'

The other stared at him, smiled broadly and folded his bare arms on the bar counter. His arms were like two great tattooed hams.

'Why, belay 'em below if it ain't Mr. Strange!' he bellowed

His watery eyes twinkled in his florid face. ' 'Ow are yer, shipmate?'

'Rolling home, you know. How's yourself?'

'All the better for seein' you!'

'Nicely put and same here,' Jimmy acknowledged.

Cicero mechanically lifted glasses while he mopped the bar.

'Any messmates with ye?' he asked.

'Over there,' Jimmy nodded. 'Sister of a chap we've waved off to a distant clime. So we need a snifter to cheer us up.'

Cicero ran a hand over his bald head. 'I'd 'ave parted me 'air if I'd known you was calling!' he guffawed. 'What'll it be?'

Jimmy gave his order. He leaned over the bar and said casually: 'By the way, how's your daughter?'

'Laura?' The smile dwindled from the other's face. 'She's — she's well enough.'

'You don't sound so sure.'

Cicero allowed himself to look worried. He said in a confiding tone:

'Truth to tell, I'm worried about 'er.'

'What's the trouble?'

'No trouble exactly — yet. But a nasty squall blowin' up, or I'm no sailor.'

'And the captain hates the sea, huh?'

'Yer durned right 'e does.' Cicero jerked his head. 'Ever 'eard of a feller named Lovell?' His voice dropped to a hoarse whisper. 'If that's his right name, but it's what he sails under.'

Jimmy nodded thoughtfully. 'Strikes a familiar chord, but I haven't *quite* got the tune. Just a minute while I take these drinks over.'

As he set the drinks down before Sandra, Jimmy wondered how a woman who could look at him with such obvious affection could yet deny him her kisses.

'That looks good,' she said.

He lifted his glass to her.

'Happy days!'

'Cheers!'

Jimmy said: 'Will you forgive me if I stagger back for a minute? Cicero's in the process of unburdening his heart to me about his wayward daughter.'

'Poor man! He does look rather worried. Don't worry about me. I'm quite cosy here.'

'Back in a minute.'

He returned to Cicero, who produced a photograph for his inspection.

'Picture o' this 'ere Lovell. Keeps it on the mantelpiece inside, she does.'

It showed a man of about thirty-five, displaying a mouthful of teeth in an arrogant smile. It was the sort of face you could see playing the pintable palaces round Soho.

Jimmy said, 'Slick-looking all right.'

' 'E's a blinkin' shark if you arsk me.'

Jimmy was trying to place the face. 'But she won't be warned off, eh?'

Cicero shook his head gravely. 'Won't listen to her old dad no more. She thinks this blighter's a ruddy wonder.' Cicero snorted. ' 'E tells 'er 'e's got a posh job in the City. Ha! Only time 'e's in the City is two in the mornin', bustin' safes!'

Jimmy said: 'You suspect him of being no better than he should be, evidently.'

'I don't like 'im, nor 'is shipmates neither.'

'You've met his friends?'

'They comes in 'ere they do every now and then, and huddles up in that corner with 'is nibs.'

'Maybe they don't want others to hear what they're talking about,' Jimmy suggested helpfully.

'Any'ow, 'e ain't no sort for young Laura. If 'er ma was 'ere — Gawd rest 'er soul — she wouldn't dare argue with 'er. Do as she was blinkin' well told she would.'

'You find her a bit of a handful, eh?'

'Oh, she's orl right really, isn't a better girl. But it's this chap.'

'Love's young dream.' Jimmy gave a heavy sigh. 'It must be difficult for you.'

'Difficult?' the other echoed. 'It's nearly drivin' me orf me ruddy rocker!' He glanced at the door. 'Take ternight, f' rinstance: she oughter be in, but she ain't. Wot's she up to? That's wot I'd like ter know.'

'I shouldn't worry too much about her.' Jimmy was anxious to return to Sandra, who was looking both beautiful and pensive in her corner. Cicero, however, was not to be restrained from unburdening his worries. 'I wouldn't mind if it was any other chap,' he went on. 'But 'im — no. I tell yer — cripes!' He broke off, his eyes popping in the direction of the swing doors. 'Don't look now — but there's one of Lovell's pals now!'

'Who is he?'

'Yeller Face wot's just come in. Been once afore 'e 'as, with Lovell.' Cicero's jaw tightened. 'Strike me mizzen-mast! 'E's gorn over ter speak ter your lady friend!'

Jimmy had registered the approach of the Chinese newcomer to Sandra with raised eyebrows. He flicked the ash off his cigarette and murmured speculatively:

'My, my, I never knew she'd any Chinese pals! Excuse me. Cicero.'

He picked up an evening paper which a customer had left folded on the bar counter. Using it as a screen, he stood within a yard of Sandra and the little Chinaman. Both of them were unconscious of his presence. Negligently he leaned against a table apparently engrossed in the racing results, with one ear taking in the yellow visitor's conversation: 'You please excuse if one sit here?' the Chinaman was asking Sandra politely.

'Why — er — yes, if you wish to,' she replied in a puzzled tone.

'Beautiful young lady not mind?' the other went on. And then in lower, more significant tones; 'I flend of Miss Lovell.'

Jimmy grinned to himself behind his newspaper as he heard her answer in puzzled confusion, 'I — I didn't catch the name. Whom did you say?'

'Miss Lovell. Beautiful lady understand?'

He leaned forward meaningly. Sandra, somewhat bewildered, and slightly alarmed, looked round for Jimmy to come to her aid. At that moment he glanced from behind the paper, gave her a quick wink and nodded imperceptibly. The Chinaman missed this byplay, and Sandra, completely at sea but anxious to play whatever part Jimmy had assigned her, turned to the yellow man.

'Why, yes, I am a friend of Mr. Lovell,' she gulped. 'Is — is anything wrong?'

'Nothing wrong. Do not disturb yourself. Just take this.' With an impassive expression he handed her a brown-paper package neatly tied with twine.

'What? No, no, this isn't for me — ' she protested

'Please, it all right,' the other interrupted.

She gave a quick glance at the newspaper behind which Jimmy was hiding. He gave no sign. She decided to carry on with the mysterious game he had started for her. She said to the Chinaman:

'Well ... if you're sure there's no mistake.'

'No mistake.' With a bland smile he rose and bowed courteously. 'Goodbye — now.' And the yellow man sidled to the doors, pushed through them and disappeared into the street.

Jimmy sat down beside Sandra. He said:

'Who's the boyfriend?'

'What a fantastic little man! And what was the idea getting me to play up to him?'

'Just a hunch I had, darling.' Casually he patted the packet she was holding. 'I get them sometimes.' His gaze flickered from her face to the package again. 'So this is the present he left for you.'

She said: 'I can't imagine what's in it.'

'Maybe something nice.'

He took it from her. 'You open it,' she said. 'I'm afraid something may jump out at me!'

'A Chinese cracker, eh?' he grinned. 'I'll take a chance.'

With a glance round to see no one was looking at them, he quickly slipped the string off the package and unwrapped the paper. He gave a little whistle and stared at the contents for a moment.

'What is it?' Sandra asked excitedly. 'Is it — dope?'

'You've been reading shilling shockers, my pet!'

'What is it, then?'

'Like to take a look-see?'

She did so and gasped.

'Five pound notes! All nice and new.'

He said: 'Yes . . . all very new.'

'Mr. Lovell is a lucky man!'

'Who?'

'Lovell. That's who the little Chinaman said they're meant for.'

Jimmy said quickly, 'Great Scotland Yard!' A sudden grin quirked the corners of his mouth. 'Which reminds me!'

'Where are you going now?' she said, somewhat petulantly. 'I don't know that I care for this drinking alone!'

'To 'phone,' he said, smiling at her fondly.

'The police?'

'However did you guess? Relax and don't worry, darling. Back in a minute.'

Cicero directed Jimmy to an automatic telephone in the passage, and after a few moments the voice of Inspector Crow sizzled over the wire like water on red-hot coals.

In his smoothest tones, Jimmy said, 'Now calm yourself. It's only me again! Or should it be I? I never can remember — '

'Hell's bells — Strange — '

'Is the name,' Jimmy completed for him, chuckling at the undisguised disfavour in the Scotland Yard man's voice. 'How are you? As if I cared!'

'Confound you! What do you want?'

'Just a word in your shell-like ear.'

'Well, I'm not in a receptive mood this evening. I've had a hard day and I'm on my way home.'

'Pity — great pity!' Jimmy commiserated. 'I was going to tell you about some counterfeit notes I've just picked up. However, if you're too tired, Inspector, you'd better toddle off to bye-byes and forget all about it.'

'Where did you find them?' rasped Crow quickly. 'Where are you speaking from?'

156

'I thought that might wake you up. Ever heard of a chap named Lovell?'

'So it is him, is it?' the other grunted.

Jimmy said: 'I didn't say so. Why? Is our Mr. Lovell the kind who goes in for that sort of thing?'

Crow scowled: 'Cut the little innocent, Strange! You know his racket as well as we do. I sometimes wonder if you don't know more than we do,' he added sourly. 'More than you should. However, one of these days you and I are going to — '

Jimmy interrupted him with elaborate politeness. 'It's awfully sweet of you to take such an interest in me — but doesn't our friend Lovell have prior claim to your attention at the moment?'

'Maybe you're right,' the other grumbled. 'I was just warning you.' He went on: 'We've had our eye on him since he came out of prison.'

'Afraid he's been returning to his wicked ways, eh?'

'I'm pretty sure he's behind the distribution of these notes that have been going around.'

'Yes, there's certainly a nice packet

waiting for him here.'

'Where?'

'The 'Queer Fish' — down by the docks. I'm 'phoning from there.'

'I know it.'

Jimmy said: 'He should be calling in to collect presently.' He paused. 'Well, I'll be getting back to my drink. So long, Inspector.'

Smiling to himself, he returned to the bar and ordered a couple more drinks. Cicero served him and gave him a searching look. But Jimmy didn't say anything, and took the drinks over to Sandra. She caught the look of amusement in his face.

'What's so funny?' she said. 'Here I'm left all alone while you run round in circles acting like something out of a thriller and don't tell me a word about it.'

'It's not been much of an evening for you,' he agreed, sitting beside her. 'But all will be revealed to you in due course.'

'Thanks very much!'

He raised his drink. 'Here's to the sweetest girl I know!'

Over the rim of her glass she said:

'You know, Jimmy, there must be something very magnetic about you — the way you always seem to attract *trouble*!'

He looked at her mouth thoughtfully.

'I wish I could attract you,' he said.

'I'm not trouble!'

'Some day, Sandra, when you're more grown-up, you're going to regret the time you wasted — '

He broke off as a tall man entered and sauntered over to the bar. His light fawn suit had built-up areas on each shoulder. He wore a snap-brim trilby aslant over one eye and a diamond pin flashed in his tie. He carried a raincoat over his arm.

' 'Evening, Cicero,' he said. 'Laura come back?'

Cicero, who'd flashed a meaning glance towards Jimmy, grunted:

' 'Evening. I thought she was with you.'

The newcomer said easily: 'Yes, I asked her to come back earlier for me. I've got here sooner than I thought. She won't be long, I expect.' He fingered the inside of his collar. 'Warm tonight. Think I'll leave my coat in your room.'

Cicero's face expressed his resentment at this condescending familiarity, but he made no reply.

'Back in a minute: Get me a double Scotch.' The other moved away, then stopped suddenly and spoke in a low voice over his shoulder. 'Who's the guy over there? With the girl?'

Cicero said: 'I dunno. Why should I?'

'Ain't seen 'em here before.' He nodded appreciatively. 'Girl looks all right.'

'Laura would be pleased yer thinks so!'

'Aw shut up! Chap can express an opinion, can't he?'

Cicero grunted non-committally.

Lovell turned back to the bar. He said: 'By the way, anyone been in for me?'

'The little Chinaman.'

'When?' — quickly.

The man behind the bar looked at him speculatively. 'Just now.'

The other frowned thoughtfully. Then: 'Did he ask for Laura?'

'Why the 'ell should 'e?'

'All right, all right! Take it easy. He went out again, eh?'

'Yus. And I wouldn't mind if others I know would foller his example!'

Lovell ignored the thrust. He said: 'Fix me that drink.' Carrying his raincoat, he went through into the little room at the back of the bar. Cicero looked after him with ill-concealed displeasure, and muttering to himself poured out the whisky. After a moment the other returned without his coat. He took his drink and sat down at a nearby table.

Jimmy, who had been surreptitiously watching him, motioned to Sandra. She followed him over to the bar. His face enigmatic, he said:

'Well . . . we must be popping, Cicero.'

Cicero looked quickly at Lovell then back to Jimmy. Instinctively he sensed something was due to happen. Soon. And Mr. Strange was to be at the back of it. He cleared his throat noisily, slapped his cloth industriously over the wet glass-stains. 'Raisin' anchor, are yer?' he said, with an enormous wink.

'Yes,' Jimmy added casually: 'Wonder if we could sail out the back way? I've a hunch someone may be arriving in a minute whom I'd rather miss.'

'Okay. Through the back room and into the passage.

'Thanks.'

'Goodbye,' Sandra smiled at him.

'Bung-o, miss. Come again.'

Only a short while after they had gone, Cicero observed two figures pushing through his swing doors. The first was bowler-hatted, bull-necked, with bushy eyebrows of a bright ginger hue. He lumbered heavily towards the bar, followed by his companion, a podgy, pale-faced individual with mild, almost aesthetic features. Brusquely the first man introduced himself to Cicero.

'I'm Inspector Crow. We're from Scotland Yard.'

Cicero stuck his lower lip out. He said: 'What do *I* do? Fall on yer neck and kiss yer?'

The Inspector's eyebrows met in a menacing line. Then, choosing to ignore the other's facetiousness, he turned on his heel and surveyed the crowded bar. In the somewhat embarrassed silence that had followed upon the detectives' entrance,

Crow indicated Lovell.

'Like a word with you,' he said.

Lovell stood up and came over with a self-confident air. 'This is an unexpected pleasure!' he grinned.

'You're Lovell, aren't you?' growled the Inspector.

'And what's it to you? What's on your mind?'

'Counterfeit notes.' Crow believed in coming to the point quickly.

Lovell said: 'Know any other funny jokes?'

The other glanced across the bar into the back room. To Cicero he said: 'I'd like to search him. In there.'

Cicero shrugged his fat shoulders. 'Go ahead.'

Jauntily, Lovell went through the bar, followed by the two detectives, and crowded into the little room. Cicero lounged in the doorway, looking on. Crow said: 'Take a look at him, Sergeant.'

A pained expression crossed Sergeant Warburton's face. He eyed Lovell's eye-catching suit and shook his head sadly. 'Dear me!' he said, in genuine distress. 'Shocking colour scheme. Now, if only you'd — '

'Search him!' rasped Crow.

Warburton sighed. 'Well, if you *insist*,' he murmured, and not without repugnance his pudgy delicate hands began to explore the sartorial monstrosity before him. Lovell raised his arms, cheerfully submitting to the search.

'I should worry.' He showed his teeth in a grin. 'You'll find nothing on me. I don't carry a thing that'd make this new suit bulge.'

After a moment Sergeant Warburton looked up. 'He's right, sir. Not a thing on him.'

Crow glowered at him in puzzlement and angry dismay. Muttering to himself, he pulled a chair to him and sat down heavily.

'You've been a bit too smart this time, copper,' Lovell jeered, adding, 'and perhaps you wouldn't mind getting off my raincoat. I didn't buy it as a cushion for suspicious-minded flatfeet!'

The detective levered himself up and pulled from beneath him the coat on which he'd inadvertently sat. He held it out to the other.

'I don't want it yet,' Lovell sneered at him. 'I'm not leaving — except in my own time.'

'You say this is yours?' Crow asked him.

'It is. Bought and paid for.' He turned to Sergeant Warburton. 'Perhaps you'd like to maul that about?' But the Sergeant's eyes were on his superior, who at that moment was extracting a bundle from a pocket. The package crackled as the Inspector examined it.

Crow said slowly: 'And this little lot would be yours too?'

He held out the roll of counterfeit notes.

'Cripes!' Lovell exclaimed inelegantly, his eyes popping. 'Where the hell did they come from?'

'That's what we're waiting for you to tell us,' said Sergeant Warburton gently.

* * *

Some time later that night Jimmy Strange replaced his telephone receiver. To Sandra,

165

snuggled in an armchair, he said:

'So the old Crow reckons he'll have the rest of Lovell's crowd roped in by midnight.'

'Is that what he's just told you?'

Jimmy nodded. He crushed his cigarette out.

'Bit of luck recognizing him from the photo Cicero showed me.'

'You must have a remarkable memory for faces,' she smiled.

He looked at her. 'Some are unforgettable,' he said softly.

She said quickly: 'And I suppose the little Chinaman was one of the gang?'

'Yes. Passing the stuff round for distribution. That's how you came to handle it. He mistook you for Laura. It was then I guessed what the game was. Glad I was able to keep the girl out of it. Little fool. Infatuated with Lovell, who was just making use of her. He's that type.'

'Very bright of you slipping the notes into his coat like that.'

He nodded absently and eyed her with a thoughtful expression.

'Could be nice having a girl infatuated with you,' he said.

From her armchair Sandra's voice was exasperatingly non-committal. 'Could be.' she said.

There was a little pause, then he sighed philosophically.

'On the other hand,' he said, 'it didn't do Lovell much good . . . '

'Or Laura!' Sandra said.

And Jimmy laughed and lit another cigarette.

6

The Brummel Snuff-Box

The *Daily Clarion* had the beat on the rest of Fleet Street over the Brummel Snuffbox story as a result of a lucky break that comes all too rarely in the life of a newspaperman.

Of the newshawks who'd been hanging round Scotland Yard Press Bureau all evening, Kelly, *Clarion* ace crime reporter happened to be last to leave. It had been a quiet night and it was late now as Kelly went out on to the misty Embankment. As the door closed behind him he paused to light a cigarette, and at that moment caught the burr-burr of a jangling telephone in the room he'd just quitted. He hesitated. Might be something, might be nothing.

He heard the muffled voice of the officer on duty answering the call, and it may have been a certain note in the man's voice or just plain reporter's instinct told him it was something.

He went back.

A few minutes later he was ringing his paper.

'Gimme the news editor.'

He was through quickly.

'Kelly here.'

'Yes, old cock?'

'Got any room for a hot exclusive?'

'How hot?'

'The famous Brummel snuff-box's been pinched.'

'The who?'

'Brummel snuff-box, ignorant! Jewel-studded, priceless relic once used by old Beau Brummel himself.'

The night editor yawned. 'Who's it belong to?'

'Lady Audrey Doone — it *did*.'

'Lady Doone, eh?' A sharpening of interest. 'Hm . . . Okay, old cock, let's have it quick.'

''Mayfair Beauty's Famous Antique Stolen — Daring Theft of Priceless Relic' — all that sort of tripe,' urged Kelly, his voice raised dramatically.

'Don't let your imagination run riot!' replied the other sarcastically through another yawn. Then added crisply: 'Better come and write the story here. Get all the dope on Lady Doone then — you've got twenty minutes before the next edition.'

Kelly rang off, and grumbling to himself about the lack of enthusiasm these so-and-so so-and-sos of news editors showed a hard-working reporter who'd just picked up an exclusive smashing story he hailed a taxi cruising slowly past and was on his way to Fleet Street.

With the result that next morning some 3,000,000 *Clarion* readers were able to devour along with their breakfasts the sensational and exclusive story of the famous snuff-box robbery.

Among which 3,000,000 two people at any rate showed only a cursory interest in the newspaper report. The one because he was more engrossed in his breakfast at the moment, and in any case crime was to him in the nature of a routine matter and nothing to miss a morsel of succulent bacon over. He was Detective-Inspector

Crow of Scotland Yard. Of whom more later.

The other's interest in crime was also of a professional nature, and while he evinced a kind of academic curiosity, he too found nothing unduly exciting in the account of the theft of the Beau Brummel relic. To say nothing of the fact that as he was reading it the telephone had rung and the voice in his ear at once drove all other thoughts but those of tenderness and loving affection from his mind.

He was Jimmy Strange. While the owner of the voice was, of course, the delectable and desirable Sandra.

Yet, before the day was out, the Brummel snuff-box affair was destined to play a far from unimportant part in the activities of both Inspector Crow and Mr. Strange. It obtruded upon Jimmy Strange's activities that afternoon in the eminently law-abiding and artistic atmosphere of the Portland Hall, that revoltingly architectural edifice of mid-Victorian proportions that is the mecca of music-lovers. Jimmy's presence in these what were for him perhaps somewhat unusual surroundings was a direct result of Sandra's telephone call earlier.

'I'm in a mood for soulful music,' she told him.

'New record of Bing Crosby, a matinée at some musical comedy, or dancing at the Gardenia Club tonight?' he'd asked.

'I mean *real* music,' she'd said, adding firmly, 'we're going to hear the symphony concert at the Portland Hall this afternoon.'

She'd rattled off various names of unpronounceable foreign origin, which he assumed were those of the composers or performers. 'Simply marvellous,' she'd enthused.

'Sounds it' — dubiously. 'I can see I'm going to have a whale of a time!'

'What you need is uplift, darling.'

'What I'll need is a row of double Scotches.'

However he had yielded to her blandishments and supported by an excellent lunch plus suitable alcoholic stimulant, here he was, with Sandra on his arm at the Portland Hall. As they made their way through the crowded foyer to their seats on the left-hand aisle, he suddenly paused and chuckled.

'Well, well!'

'What, what?' queried Sandra, then she followed the direction of his gaze. He was smiling at a little individual who sat in the same row that they were approaching. Their seats were next to his. The man glanced up with a grin of recognition as Jimmy took his place next to him.

'Hello, there!'

'Never thought you were a lover of music,' Jimmy said. He introduced him to Sandra, hesitating over his name in time for him to supply it himself. He wasn't quite sure what name the little man was currently travelling under.

'Willis — Frankie Willis. Pleased to meet you . . . ' And he leaned forward to eye Sandra with openly warm admiration, turning to Jimmy with a look of envious respect. 'Oh,' he said, 'I often enjoy an earful at this dump. Helps me to think, y'know.'

'About what?' Jimmy grinned.

The other smiled slyly in return.

'My — er — business.'

Jimmy smiled. 'I see.'

'Yes,' Willis went on blandly, 'I sits back with my peepers shut and listens. Amazin' what a chap can — er — work out listening to music.'

'It must be. Tell me more.'

Willis glanced at Sandra. 'Sure it won't bore the lady?'

She shook her head. 'Not at all. Much better to chat now *before* the music starts.'

'You're right there,' the man nodded. 'Well, y'see this kind of music sort of soothes me. And when I'm soothed my old brain-box starts to tick over like one o'clock — ' He broke off suddenly. 'Strike a light! What's *he* doing here?'

Jimmy looked at the dark, slim man who had just sat down a couple of rows in front. He raised an eyebrow at Willis, who wore a puzzled expression on his hatchet face and said, 'Maybe he likes music too.'

'Not him,' the other said decisively.

'You know him?'

'I know his racket.'

'He sounds rather intriguing,' said Sandra.

'It all depends on what you mean by 'intriguing',' and Willis breathed one word in Jimmy's ear: 'Blackmail.'

Jimmy regarded the dark man with fresh interest.

'Mason, his name is,' his informant volunteered. 'Paul Mason, and is he tough.'

Sandra said: 'What do you think would have brought him here, then? Or has he come to be soothed, too?'

Willis grinned slyly at her. Then his face became serious again.

'Beats me,' he said.

'Evidently looking for somebody,' Jimmy said.

'Glad *I* ain't that somebody!'

Sandra said quietly, 'Well, right at this moment he seems to be showing considerable interest in that woman over there. Look, she's turned round and seen him — ' She broke off with a little exclamation. 'Good Lord! It's Lady Doone.'

'What, the one who's had the robbery?' said Willis quickly.

Jimmy nodded.

The other went on, a note of excitement in his voice: 'Blimey! He's going over to her.'

But the dark man paused when he reached the aisle. He stood for a moment staring at the woman who was looking back at him from a few seats away. Then he swung on his heel and walked quickly to an exit at the side of the hall.

Sandra touched Jimmy's arm.

'Look at her face,' she breathed. 'Scared stiff!'

Jimmy nodded non-committally.

Willis was muttering: 'What the hell can he want with her?'

There came a sudden burst of applause as a tall individual stepped on to the concert platform and took his place before the orchestra, which had been tuning up and preparing for his arrival.

'Ah, here's the bloke who waves the little stick,' said Willis, and leaned back expectantly in his seat.

Jimmy saw Lady Doone rise hurriedly and move towards the aisle. Her eyes never left the exit through which the dark man had disappeared. With nervous haste she gained the door and went through.

Jimmy murmured to Sandra: 'Think I'd like a quiet smoke.'

She had seen the woman's sudden departure, and she gave him an understanding nod. 'Never will learn to mind your own business, will you?'

He grinned and stood up.

She leaned up and whispered, 'One thing before you go: who exactly is your music-loving friend?'

He glanced at Frankie Willis, who had his eyes already closed in relaxed anticipation.

'A cardsharper,' Jimmy said into Sandra's pretty little ear.

'Really, now,' she said. 'What quaint people you know!'

As he made his way after Lady Doone, the conductor tapped peremptorily with his baton, and the introductory swell of the music rose and followed him through the side exit.

He paused for a moment. The wide corridor appeared deserted. Then suddenly he caught the sound of murmuring voices a few yards away. He listened intently and located them behind one of the massive pillars near by. He moved quietly in its direction.

The woman was saying, her voice raised slightly in protest:

'But you're powerless. You've given me back the photograph.'

Came the man's smooth reply:

'The *print*, yes.'

She obviously did not grasp the implication in his tone, and Jimmy, on the other side of the pillar, and to whom the dark man's scheme was immediately as obvious as it was dirty, marvelled that anyone could be so dumb and trusting as she sounded. He thought grimly: It must have been like stealing candy from a baby.

'The — the print?' she queried.

'I still hold the negative.'

Followed a little pause, during which Jimmy could almost hear the penny drop. She gave a low, convulsive gasp, and her voice was charged with loathing.

'*You devil!*'

'I'm glad you understand,' he said coolly.

'I won't give you any money! I can't'

— she hit a high, hysterical note — 'you know I can't!'

'Pipe down,' he said brutally. 'The people in there want to listen to the music! Just five thousand, that's all, to tide me over — '

'But you've got the snuff-box — '

'It's too hot to dispose of yet. I didn't realize there'd be such a song-and-dance over the thing. Meantime — well, I've got to live, you know. Haven't I?' Jimmy could almost see his smile that derisively mocked her.

'I can't give you money,' she reiterated. 'That way my husband would know.'

'All right,' he said thoughtfully. 'You'd better get back now. After it's over, come along to my flat — 6, Park House, off Piccadilly. We'll have a talk and maybe think up some way for you to find the ready cash — '

'There isn't a way,' she said wearily.

'We'll see. I'll beat it now. At my flat, then?'

'I shan't come,' she answered, suddenly defiant.

There was no reply for a moment.

179

Then his soft laughter, and:

'I think you will. I mean, it *is* rather an interesting photograph.'

Jimmy manoeuvred himself further out of sight round the pillar as the man went by. He waited and heard the woman murmuring to herself chokingly. She was obviously making a tremendous effort to prevent herself breaking down. He decided this might be the moment to do something. He moved forward.

'Anything I can do?'

She gave a gasp and faced him.

Seeing her at close quarters like this, Jimmy understood why the columnists and society magazines described her as 'the loveliest lady in London', and all the rest of the superlatives. She certainly was an eyeful. A bit on the tall side for him, he thought. He liked 'em to come up to his shoulder — but her beautiful greenish eyes were on a level with his.

'It's nothing,' she said. 'I'm — I'm quite all right.'

'You seemed a little distressed,' he said easily.

She gave him a stiff little smile and

made as if to pass him. 'I — I was feeling a little faint. But I'm better now. I think I'll go back to the concert.'

He nodded, then added very quietly:

'But I wouldn't go and see Mr. Mason afterwards.'

Her face as she swung round was drained of colour.

'How do you — ' She gasped and stared at him, her question left trailing in the air.

He went on gently: 'I mean, he's not very nice to know.'

Her gaze went past him to the pillar. He smiled and answered the query in her look.

'Afraid I've been guilty of a little eavesdropping. Rotten thing to do, I know, but then — people's morals aren't what they were. Or are they?' He took out his cigarette case. 'Matter of fact,' he said, eyeing her levelly, 'I happened to come out for a smoke. Will you have one? Steady the nerves a bit.'

She took a cigarette and he lit it, then his own.

'Then I heard you and Mason having a

little chat, and — well, I listened-in.'

'I'm sure you must have found our conversation most illuminating.'

'Is that meant as a rebuke or just a passing remark?'

She drew a deep breath and said in a tired voice, 'Does it matter?'

'But definitely, Lady Doone. I'd hate to feel someone so charming had taken a dislike to me.' He added pensively, 'People don't as a rule.'

'I see you know who I am. Who are you?'

He told her. He said, through a cloud of cigarette smoke:

'I take it Mr. Mason's got a snapshot taken on the beach at Brighton or something which features you, and which he's threatening to show your husband?' His tone was deliberately light, but his eyes regarding her were narrow and speculative. After all, she may wear a title, but she could be as crooked as a corkscrew as well. There might be more in all this than he knew. She might be double-crossing Paul Mason, or her husband, or both. Though he was pretty sure she was on the level.

Her answer told him.

'It was a silly party I went to. I don't remember how the photograph was taken. I never even remembered there was a camera. Paul Mason was there — I'd met him before with the same crowd — and he showed me the photo about a week later.'

He shook his head almost pityingly. It was the oldest trick and she had fallen for it. He decided she was not a particularly intelligent type, but all the same he felt sorry for her. And she was very beautiful.

He said: 'So you gave him the Beau Brummel snuff-box in return for the picture?'

'I couldn't pay him the money he asked, my husband would have found out.'

He nodded quickly and went on: 'And pretended it had been pinched' — he corrected himself with a smile — 'stolen?'

'Yes.'

'Which is our friend's cue to enter to tell you he still has the negative and some hard cash would come in handy.'

'What a fool I must look to you,' she said, in a low voice.

'The way you look takes my breath away,' he said at once, flashing her his charming smile. Then said grimly: 'And so does the way you've been fooling around!'

She was silent.

He chuckled. 'It's quite simple, really. Or will be if you do as I tell you.'

'What?' she asked hesitantly.

'Listen, you beautiful but stupid character from a Mayfair cocktail party, and let my words of wisdom sink into that elegant nut of yours . . . just go back and enjoy the concert.'

She stared at him, her lovely eyes wide in incredulous fascination.

'When it's through,' he proceeded smoothly, 'wait by the main booking-office till I turn up — take a good look at me so's you'll remember my pretty mug! I shan't be late, and then you can run along home.'

'But I — I — '

He took her arm and urged her towards the door.

'Come on, now.'

She obeyed him as if in a trance, pausing to begin to ask:

'Yes, but what are you going to do . . . ?'

He said easily:

'You've missed quite a bit of the concert, you don't want to miss any more, do you?' — and opened the door. The music flowed out to them in engulfing waves.

'Pretty, isn't it?' he said, smiling, and motioned her forward.

She went in, then turned to him. 'What are you going to — ' she began again, in an anxious whisper.

He shut the door in her lovely face.

'Taxi, sir?' said the large commission-aire, as he reached the wide steps leading from the foyer into the street.

'You read my thoughts like a book!'

The man bounced ahead of him, and a taxi was drawing up to the kerb as Jimmy came out.

'Didn't yer like the music, sir?' the commissionaire asked solicitously, as he held open the taxi door.

'Er — not very much.'

The other shook his head sympathetically. 'I can't get on with that 'ighbrow stuff neither. No tune. Gimme somethink you can whistle!'

Jimmy nodded and produced two concert-ticket counterfoils, which he handed him plus a generous tip. 'These are my seats. You'll find a lady in one of 'em — next to the empty one I've just left. Slip in and tell her I've got a headache and am taking it for a walk. Savvy?'

'Leave it ter me, sir.' And as Jimmy got into the taxi: 'Where to, sir?'

'Park House, off Piccadilly. Quick!'

* * *

Twenty minutes later Inspector Crow slammed down his receiver with an irritable grunt and leaned back heavily in his chair. A worried frown drew his beetling ginger brows together. After a moment he lifted the receiver again.

'Tell Sergeant Warburton I want him,' he rasped, adding: 'and tell him I want him today!'

He pushed back his chair and lumbered to the window, frowning at the mid-afternoon sky. From Whitehall came the rumble of traffic, its monotony broken irregularly by the strident notes of motor hooters. Big Ben struck the quarter, and from somewhere down river a tug siren gave a thin wail.

Came a tap on the door.

'Come in!' barked the Inspector, and Sergeant Warburton shut the door behind him and advanced into the room.

The Inspector gave him a bitter look, sighed heavily, ambled back to his desk and slumped heavily into his chair. Warburton stood patiently, his expression austere and immobile. His superior's moody irritability and, to his mind, utterly irrational outburst of rage left him as unmoved as did his glowering silences. Despite his aesthetic features, the Sergeant's skin was reasonably thick, and — apart from a nervous schoolgirl blush which, on occasions of embarrassment he had so far been unable to control — Inspector Crow's tantrums and bull-like bellowing caused him no apparent distress. His resilience to recrimination, his capacity for absorbing insults remained as great as ever.

In fact, he had long realized that life without Crow with his blustering and explosive personality would be very dull. Hardly worth living, really. He allowed this reflection to soften his expression as he considered the Inspector. Yes, he thought, you might say there was something almost lovable about the old unprintable.

His contemplation was rudely shattered by a bellow from the object of his warm regard.

'Don't stand there drooling at me like a ruddy cow! I sent for you because we've got a job on.'

'Quite, sir.'

Inspector Crow scratched his heavy, deeply cleft chin thoughtfully. 'At least, I think we have.' He screwed his face as if he'd eaten a particularly sour apple and ground out between set teeth, 'Strange has been on the 'phone.'

Sergeant Warburton's features brightened with interest.

'Jimmy Strange, sir — not again!'

He subsided beneath the other's brooding glare.

'Says he's got the Brummel snuff-box — or, at any rate told us exactly where we can put our hands on it.'

'Really, sir, that's very intriguing. The snuff-box is a most valuable relic, I understand. Jewel-encrusted and most beautifully designed. Used by the great dandy himself; and had been in the possession of the Doone family for many years. In fact, it's said Beau Brummel himself presented it to a Doone for — '

'I've read the newspapers too!' snarled Crow.

'Quite, sir.' He coughed delicately, and asked politely, 'What suggestions had Mr. Strange to offer with regard to returning the relic to its rightful owner?'

'Why the hell don't you speak plain ruddy English?' railed the other. 'Blathering on as if you'd swallowed the blasted dictionary!'

Warburton sighed, and mentally rejected his earlier notion that there was anything lovable about the Inspector. The latter went on: 'This damned Strange man said he was 'phoning from the flat of the chap who'd pinched the snuff-box — and the chap is Paul Mason.'

The Sergeant gave an indulgent little smile.

'That's ridiculous,' he said. 'Paul Mason is a blackmailer. Robbery has never been his line.'

'Exactly what I was coming to — if only you'd let me get a word in edgeways!' Crow stuck out his lower lip and pulled at it slowly. 'Point is, Strange has never given us a wrong tip-off to date,' he muttered. 'Only reason why I think there might be something in this, in spite of Mason's record being entirely blackmail.'

'Perhaps he's decided a change might do him good.'

Inspector Crow grunted. 'You know as well as I do a crook always sticks to his last.' The Sergeant nodded.

The other resumed: 'All the same, this may be an exception that proves the rule, and — it's about time Mason was pulled in. Doesn't matter if it's for theft or his old racket.'

'If Strange named him, it would

certainly seem as if he has good reason for it.'

'That's my idea.'

And, his mind made up, he rose from his desk abruptly and reached for his bowler hat. 'Come on,' he growled.

'Where to, sir, exactly?'

'Park House, off Piccadilly. That's where he 'phoned from.'

As they went out of the office, Warburton asked precisely:

'Did he explain how he came to be in Mason's flat, sir, and was able to make a telephone call to you from there?'

'Obviously because he'd got in there while Mason was out, you fool!'

And Sergeant Warburton blushed a delicate shade of pink and hurried after the other, lumbering ahead like a bowler-hatted elephant.

The Inspector's judicious deduction was not altogether correct, however, for at the precise moment of his voicing it Paul Mason was *in*.

Jimmy Strange, in fact, was listening intently from the sitting room as the door of the flat opened and closed, and a man's voice spoke endearingly to his companion whose feminine tones were equally endearing.

Paul Mason, no doubt, plus a cutie, returned to pass an agreeable hour until the time of his appointment with Lady Doone.

Returned, too, somewhat earlier than Jimmy had hoped!

He'd only a few moments ago replaced the receiver after telephoning Inspector Crow. Up till now everything had gone very nicely. The lock had given him practically no trouble at all, and he'd made a rapid but very thorough search of the flat undisturbed. His shrewd eyes and swift expert fingers had presently been rewarded by the discovery of (a) the incriminating negative, and (b) the Beau Brummel snuff-box.

The first he had pocketed, the second left where it was — later to indicate its exact hiding-place to Crow over the telephone.

All this had been executed with his characteristic neatness and with scrupulous care that Mr. Mason's sensibilities concerning the sanctity of his home and personal belongings should in no way be outraged.

So dexterous was his touch, the aforementioned gentleman would not have the slightest inkling that so much as a fly's wing had rustled the air of his charming flat or its contents.

Which was ever the way of Jimmy Strange in such matters.

And now, having set the rest of the operation he had in mind snugly in motion, he was just about to emulate the Arabs and their tent-folding talents and as silently push off when he'd heard that scrape of the key in the lock.

There was no time to do anything except some extremely snappy thinking. In his case, thought and action were as good as simultaneous.

As the front door closed behind the newcomers, he flopped into the most comfortable chair, snapped on the radio-set at his elbow, grabbed a magazine and leant back luxuriously, negligently flipping the pages.

The radio burst forth into the room

with the crash of some symphonic climax. Jimmy's tensed ear caught a quick feminine gasp from the little hall, and a sharp exclamation by the man; Next moment the man was in the room, his companion close beside him.

'What the hell's this mean?'

Jimmy raised an inquiring eye over his magazine as the demand cracked at him. With a somewhat vague smile he put down the magazine and stood up. He began to speak, then with a finger raised apologetically, turned and switched the radio off.

'Didn't realize I had it on so loud,' he said to Mason.

There was a moment's silence, during which Jimmy made a swift appraisal of the girl. What he saw he liked. Sultry type, with ripe red lips and satisfactorily curvaceous. Decidedly his cup of tea. She was staring at him with a mixture of interest and suspicion. In an effort to change her look to one solely of interest, he gave her the benefit of his most charming smile.

He was prevented from observing her

reaction, however, by her companion, who thrust forward threateningly.

'Cut the funny stuff!' he snapped. 'Who are you?'

Jimmy reached for his inside pocket. The girl gave a gasp of apprehension, while the man tensed as if to spring at him.

'Sorry if I startled you,' Jimmy apologized to the girl, producing his cigarette case and flipping it open. 'As you see, it is nothing more lethal than a cigarette.' He extended the case to her, but she shook her head.

'No?' And studiously ignoring the other, he took one himself.

Through a cloud of cigarette smoke he addressed Mason coolly:

'I don't think we need go into who I am for the moment. What is more interesting is I know who you are. I also know you know Lady Doone.'

The man started visibly. Then his face hardened and his eyes became slits. He said: 'Maybe I'm a little dumb, but I haven't any idea what you're yapping about.'

Jimmy drew a long sigh. 'Come, come,'

he protested, patiently amiable. 'I hope you're not going to be obstructive. You, I feel sure, are a businessman, which suits me. So let's get down to business. Business concerning a certain snuff-box of not inconsiderable worth.'

Mason's expression remained unchanged. Jimmy noted that so far as the girl was concerned every word was completely over her head.

He said to the man: 'As you will no doubt have heard, this valuable antique has been stolen. While I hasten to reassure you,' he went on easily, 'that I don't for a moment suspect you of having anything to do with the theft — '

'Thanks!'

Jimmy grinned. Did he detect a slight expression of relief in those narrowed eyes? 'Nevertheless, it occurs to me you might know something of its present whereabouts,' he murmured urbanely. 'If — by any possible chance — you do, then the insurance company concerned would be interested to make you an offer if you could — er — influence its safe return to Lady Doone. Five thousand pounds was the price the company have in mind with, needless to say, no questions asked.'

He tapped the ash off his cigarette and waited.

After a moment:

'Supposing I could do something to help Lady Doone over her unfortunate loss?' Mason said cautiously. 'I'm not saying I could, get that straight — how do I know I wouldn't get mixed up with the police over it?'

Jimmy, who'd been regarding the girl with unqualified approval, turned to him.

He said smoothly: 'As a practical man, you'll appreciate that all the company I — er — represent are interested in is the recovery of the snuff-box and so save themselves a packet. As for me, I'm in this for the cut they'll give me when I deliver the goods. I might add,' he said, examining his nails ostentatiously, 'that I haven't any particular wish to get mixed up with the busies, either.'

His veiled admittance of a murky past caused Mason to glance at him sharply, interest taking the place of suspicion in his eyes.

'Anyway,' said Jimmy negligently, 'think it over. No hurry. I'll drop in later for your answer.'

'Speaking of dropping in,' said the other heavily, 'perhaps you wouldn't mind explaining how you dropped in here while I was out.'

Jimmy chuckled. He said expansively:

'For a moment I thought you were going to ask me a really embarrassing question,' he said, 'such as how did I guess you might know something about Lady Doone's snuff-box? Or how did I know you knew Lady Doone! Questions I'd have been unable to answer without giving away professional secrets. But how I got in here is simple: I just walked in.'

'That door's got a lock on it.'

Jimmy blew a cloud of cigarette smoke ceilingwards with studied nonchalance.

'What's a locked door between friends?' he said.

Mason stared at him thoughtfully. He appeared to be satisfied with both what he'd been told and what he'd been left to infer. He said slowly, 'All right, smartie, perhaps I might be able to help you. Five thousand, did you say?'

Jimmy nodded.

'Okay,' the other said. 'Be here this evening, say around seven, and I'll have some news for you maybe. You won't have to demonstrate your tricks on the door,' he added, with a thin smile. 'I'll be waiting for you.'

'Anything you say,' Jimmy said agreeably.

At the door he turned to the sultry one.

'In case you're interested, darling, you can find me almost any night propping up the bar at 'Joe's Place', in Greek Street — '

Mason moved towards him with an indignant growl. Jimmy murmured disarmingly: 'Just taking care of the next evening when you may be too busy and she'll be lonely.' And he flashed her a devastating smile.

'Get on your way!' Mason snarled, and pulled at his shoulder — which he shouldn't have done, because Jimmy was never the one to let anyone push him around. He was going anyway, but he paused to regard the other with narrowed eyes that were suddenly glittering dangerously.

Unfortunately — for Mason — that gentleman disregarded the warning light. He lugged more angrily at Jimmy's shoulder.

That was the last thing he was to remember for the next twenty minutes. Jimmy's fist seemed to travel no more than six inches before it connected with the other's jaw, but the effect was electrical. There was a teeth-rattling crack as bone met bone and Mason slid gracefully to the floor.

The girl gave a little scream, and Jimmy glanced at her, then at the crumpled figure.

'Dear me,' he murmured apologetically. 'I shouldn't have done that.'

'You've knocked him unconscious,' she said unnecessarily.

He nodded sadly. Then looked at his watch. From past experience of the effect of the wallop he carried he calculated Mason should be coming round just about the time Inspector Crow would arrive at the flat. To the girl he said philosophically:

'Too bad. Nothing I can do about it

except take care not to be here when he comes to!' He glanced at her. 'And you?'

She looked hesitantly from him to Mason and back again.

'He'll be all right,' he assured her, 'but not exactly in a loving mood when he wakes up.' He paused and looked at her expectantly. 'I *could* see you into a taxi.'

She stared at him unblinkingly, her sultry eyes glowing, her white teeth biting her full lower lip pensively. Then, with a little smile she took his arm and they went out.

As they drove off in the taxi Jimmy was sharing with her as far as the Portland Hall, he glanced back through the window to see a speeding police-car pull up outside Park House. Inspector Crow climbed out heavily and lumbered inside, followed by Sergeant Warburton. He grinned to himself. The Inspector was on the job plenty early!

The girl glanced at him from his shoulder.

'What's the joke?' she asked.

His arm, casually protective, arranged itself so that she somehow found it easier to nestle more closely against his comforting shoulder. He said:

'Just the thought of our mutual friend's surprise when he opens his eyes.'

'And finds no one there to comfort him, you mean?'

'That's roughly what I mean,' he grinned, not batting an eyelid.

Jimmy Strange got out at the concert hall, having arranged to renew the girl's acquaintance at a later and more convenient date. He tipped the driver somewhat extravagantly — he was in that sort of mood — and the taxi took the girl on to her destination.

The concert had not long ended, a dwindling stream of people were trickling out of the hall. Out of the corner of his eye Jimmy caught sight of Sandra with Frankie Willis beside her. They were looking round expectantly. Jimmy's conscience gave a twinge as he went over — Sandra didn't look as if she'd had a wonderful afternoon exactly.

'The amount of cigarettes you must have smoked, it's a wonder you aren't dead from nicotine poisoning,' she greeted him, acidly reminding him of the excuse he'd given for leaving her. And added: 'Which mightn't have been a bad idea, either!'

'I'm sorry, darling,' he apologized, 'but I got a little involved.'

Willis said: 'Find out anything about Mason and Lady Doone?'

'A bit.'

Sandra caught the glint in his eye, the tiny triumphant smile that quirked the corners of his mouth. She sighed and said:

'One of these days you'll pop out for a quick smoke, and that'll be the last I'll have seen of you. You won't come back alive.'

Willis winked at her. 'To me he looks the sort of chap who'd always come back — to you.'

Jimmy chuckled.

Sandra gave him a long look but made no further comment.

'Thanks for taking care of her for me — ' Jimmy was saying to Willis, when Sandra with a nod towards the booking-office cut in:

'Here's your Lady Doone looking for someone. Could it be you?'

'I won't be a minute, darling,' Jimmy said.

The woman stared at him anxiously as he crossed over to her.

'I — I wondered if perhaps you wouldn't turn up,' she said in a low voice.

'The Strange Service never fails,' he grinned at her. 'This, Lady Doone, is for you.' He handed her the negative he'd found in Mason's flat.

She looked at it unbelievingly. He said: 'That the little thing you were needing?'

She nodded. When at last she found her voice it was full of emotion. 'How — how can I ever thank you?'

'You'll be getting the snuff-box back via Scotland Yard. This evening probably.'

Her green eyes were wide in wonder.

'But how did you — ?'

'If I told you the truth, you'd never believe me,' he said easily. 'And I don't tell lies — at least, not much. So why worry?' He took her arm. She was still in very much of a daze as he impelled her towards the street, saying: 'Now, let's see about getting you a taxi . . . '

He was back in a minute.

'Well, that's that,' he said to Sandra.

She eyed him steadily. 'So glad you've packed her off all nice and cosy.' Her voice was like ice. 'I think perhaps *I'll* be getting along. No — I'll find my own taxi, thank you. And thank you, too, for a most enjoyable afternoon!'

And with a flashing smile at Willis she was gone.

Jimmy stared after her blankly.

'Blimey!' said Willis. 'Talk about jealous. She must be in love with you or somethink!'

Jimmy frowned. It had been a pretty grim party for Sandra as it had turned out, he knew. And Lady Doone was very attractive — though Sandra needn't have worried about that. However, there was nothing he could do about it except wait till she'd cooled off and phone her. He'd think of something special to give her to make up for what had happened.

Willis suddenly nudged him.

'See this notice?' he said. 'This here

concert was broadcast this afternoon!' He grinned widely. 'Now, if only you and she had stayed *at home* and listened in, think of the heap of trouble you'd have saved yourself. Lovers' tiff and all!'

7

The Girl on the Embankment

Inspector Crow glowered at Sergeant Warburton. 'When did this report come in?'

'Three minutes ago, sir.'

Crow drew his ginger eyebrows together. 'It may be three minutes too late.'

'I thought it was urgent, sir, that's why I — '

'Ruddy urgent!' the other interrupted him. 'Come on.'

As he lumbered along the corridor, the Inspector fired a series of questions at Sergeant Warburton, who had almost to break into a run in order to keep up with his superior.

'Did the porter of the flats say at what time he saw the men drive off?'

'At 6.50 p.m.,' said Warburton in his precise tones, 'some ten minutes before he 'phoned. Which means,' he added helpfully, 'that the kidnapping must have occurred just over thirteen minutes ago.'

'You'll be telling me two and two make four next!' snarled Inspector Crow. 'Why didn't the porter 'phone earlier?'

Blushing slightly at the rebuke, the Sergeant answered: 'He said he didn't realize at once what had happened. He noticed that the men were carrying something bundled in a blanket, but that it might be a child didn't enter his head until well after the car had disappeared.'

The Inspector grunted. 'Then?'

'He went up to Halloran's flat and found out that the child was missing. He 'phoned us at once.'

'Has he got the number of the car?'

'Afraid not, sir. I asked him that, of course. All he could say was that it was a saloon and black.'

'So are a thousand other cars!'

Crow pushed open a door marked 'Patrol'. He gave rapid instructions to an officer on duty at a desk fitted with a microphone. The officer scribbled as quickly as the Inspector spoke, and in a moment was himself speaking incisively into the instrument before him.

'Calling all stations . . . all stations . . . Patrols all districts . . . Keep a lookout black saloon car, probably two or three occupants, men, proceeding from Mayfair district with boy aged four years, believed kidnapped. Child American: hazel eyes, straight fair hair, wearing pyjamas, dressing gown, wrapped in blanket . . . '

Inspector Crow turned to Warburton.

'Wait around for any reports to come through. Bring any news straight to my office. Make it snappy — so long as you don't strain yourself!'

'Very good, sir,' said the Sergeant primly.

Crow returned to his office and attended to the business that had been occupying him until he received the report of the kidnapping. Some fifteen minutes later the telephone jangled on his desk.

'Sergeant Warburton, sir, speaking from the patrol-room — '

'Yes, what's the news?'

'Only negative reports, sir, but I thought I'd ring you — '

'What d'you mean — negative?'

'Nothing, sir. Nil. No results. No trace of the car. Just vanished into the night, sir,' he added poetically.

'I wish you'd follow it!' rasped Crow irritably. 'What the hell d'you want to 'phone me for if nothing's happened? I told you to let me know the moment there was any news. Wasting my time — '

'If I may interrupt you for a moment, sir, the reason for my telephoning you is as follows: four minutes ago — four and a *half* it would be now — patrol car A.16 picked up a black saloon along the Chelsea Embankment. There was only one occupant, and they checked up the gentleman. I just felt you might be intrigued to know his identity.'

'Give me three guesses,' growled the Inspector, with heavy sarcasm. 'Was it the Commissioner?'

'Oh no, sir.'

'Then who the hell was it?' roared Crow, completely losing his patience. 'What d'you think we're playing at, some ruddy quiz game? Who was the blasted man?'

'Jimmy Strange, sir.'

Inspector Crow winced visibly. 'Him!' He gave an exclamation of disgust. 'That damned man haunts me. I suppose,' he said, with a sneer, 'the patrol asked his advice about finding the kid?'

'I think not, as a matter of fact,' said the other, then added, 'though now you come to mention it, sir, perhaps it mightn't have been a bad idea.'

The Inspector's only response was to crash down his receiver with a force sufficient almost to crack the instrument in two.

* * *

Jimmy Strange, having satisfied the officers of patrol car A.16 that he was not, in fact, three men masquerading as one, and that the object in the back of his car was nothing more incriminating than a bottle of whisky, proceeded blithely on his way along the Chelsea Embankment.

He might have been curious as to why Scotland Yard was throwing out a dragnet, except that tonight he had something more important on his mind. He was on his way to meet Sandra.

He was driving along a stretch of the Embankment, which was particularly deserted when he suddenly braked to a stop, jumped out of his car, and leapt across the pavement. He was only just in time to grasp the shoulder of the girl as she began to climb the parapet.

'Sure you can swim?' he asked laconically.

She turned and tried to wrench free.

'Let me go! Let me go!'

He chuckled easily. 'I'll bet you *can't* swim a stroke. A fine thing. And I'd have to jump in after you — '

She was sobbing hysterically.

'Please let me go. I know what I'm doing — '

Jimmy went on banteringly:

'I, who like to take my baths *hot*, let me tell you — '

Now she broke down utterly. She leant against the parapet and sobbed unrestrainedly.

A girl in tears naturally aroused Jimmy's most protective instincts, especially if the girl was attractive as this one was. He had glimpsed her face in the light of the street-lamp, and though it was white and strained with anguish, and her eyes disfigured with weeping, undoubtedly she was pretty . . .

He went on talking in a light, friendly tone:

'Besides,' he argued, 'supposing *I* can't swim, either? Dammit, I might easily drown!'

He chuckled and tilted her chin up. forcing her to look at him.

'Come on, kid,' he said. 'Take it easy. Relax. Listen, tell you what — let's you and me get together and talk this over, eh? I know a quiet little bar where we can fix ourselves up with a drink, and you can tell me your troubles and I'll tell you mine. Then we'll have a couple more, and, anyway, we'll cut out the swimming practice for tonight. Me, I could use a drink right now. Come on.'

She clung to his arm like a frightened child as he helped her into his car. In a few moments they were in the cosy 'snug' of the 'Seven Stars'. Somewhere a radio was playing treacly dance music, suitably sweetened to the popular taste.

She sank into a chair, trembling, and shakily took off her somewhat severe black hat and pressed clenched hands to her forehead. The light caught her ash-blonde hair. She was young and — Jimmy was pleased to note — very pretty, despite her tear-stained pallor. Her name, she'd told him, was Helen Carlton. He'd said it was a nice name, with the mental reservation that it might be a phoney invented for his benefit; you never could tell.

When he handed her the brandy, she sipped it and, choking, grimaced.

He grinned at her encouragingly.

'Feel better?'

'A little.' She blinked up at him uncertainly. 'You've been awfully kind.'

He shrugged off her gratitude.

'It's just a way I have. Don't let it bother you.' He eased himself into a chair beside her. 'What's on your mind? A man?'

She smiled wanly and shook her head. He eyed her over his glass. She was well if not expensively dressed. Her clothes were quiet, but obviously she wasn't poor. Her voice was nice. He figured she might be a private secretary or something in that line.

'Not a man, eh? And you don't look as if you're hard up.'

For answer she pulled a crumpled package from her coat pocket. He raised an eyebrow and saw that it was a roll of banknotes.

She said: 'There's two thousand pounds here. I ought to — to — burn it . . . '

He took a drink and merely said: 'Lots of people do — figuratively.'

'You don't understand,' she insisted. 'It's — it's bad money!' Her voice was low and charged with self-loathing. He glanced at the notes speculatively, then at her.

'Slush?' he asked, then smiled apologetically. 'Pardon me — I mean, is it counterfeit?'

'No, no — it's real enough. It's the way I got it. I've been rotten and despicable — but I didn't realize — it didn't seem so bad at the time. And then — afterwards — when they'd taken the child, I knew what a terrible thing I'd done — '

'Take it easy a minute. What — what child?'

'The Hallorans' baby boy. I'm his nurse. I told them where the child slept and — and left a window open — ' She plunged on breathlessly, as if by making full confession she could in some way expiate the wrong she had committed.

He regarded her with narrowed eyes.

'They promised not to harm the child,' she said, as if his unblinking scrutiny demanded some defence, however pitiful, of her action. 'I wanted to tell the police it was my fault, but I couldn't — I couldn't, I was too scared of going to prison — '

She broke off to bury her face in her hands, sobbing unrestrainedly.

His voice had a chill in it. 'Seems it wouldn't have helped if you *had* said anything — you don't sound as if you know where they've taken the kid.'

'But his father will call in Scotland Yard right away. They'll be hunting for him now.'

He smiled grimly to himself as he recalled his encounter with the patrol car.

Scotland Yard were on the job all right!

He said: 'Halloran's an American, eh? Plenty of dough — '

'Oh, yes.'

She took the cigarette he offered her. He lit it, then his own.

'Wonder if old Crow's heading the baby-hunt,' he mused through a cloud of cigarette smoke.

'Who?'

He shrugged evasively. 'Just someone I know.'

She was wringing her hands in anguish.

'Supposing they find out about me? Oh, why did I do it?'

'It wouldn't be something to do with the money they paid you?' he observed cynically.

She bowed her head beneath the implied contempt in his tone. 'I must have been mad. I don't want the money now,' she burst out. 'It's blood money!'

He said grimly: 'It certainly will be if — well, if anything happens to the kid.'

'Don't, don't! I can't bear to think about it.'

He eyed her for a moment, then placed

a hand on her quivering shoulder.

'Now listen. You've got to pull yourself together. Frankly, I think you've been more of a fool than a crook, and I'm sorry for you.'

'I wish I were dead!' she wailed. 'I wish I were dead!'

Jimmy sighed patiently. 'I might be agreeing with you, if I didn't hope you'll be more use to me alive. Come on, now — what I want is for you to try and remember anything which might help put us on the track of these men.'

She said slowly: 'There's nothing. I used to meet one — the dark one with the accent — in the park, when I took Sammy out. Then, later, I met the other man with him. At the Regent Hotel cocktail bar.'

He nodded, and she went on:

'We just fixed up how I was to let this other man into the nursery — and he gave me some money, and that was all.'

'No mention of where they planned to hide the kid?' he queried. 'Cottage in the country, or — or . . . ?'

'Nothing — '

Jimmy leaned forward.

'Think hard,' he urged her. 'Think damned hard.'

'I — I can't remember.' She appeared to be desperately searching her memory for anything that might offer a clue.

'Wait a minute — '

He watched her expectantly.

'He had to telephone — that time at the hotel — and he asked the dark one the number, and he said Wharfside 2020 — I remember because twenty's my age — '

'Wharfside 2020. Sure?'

She nodded emphatically. 'I'm sure.'

Jimmy finished his drink and stood up. 'Let's find a 'phone.'

He found a callbox near by and, while the girl waited outside, dialled the number she'd given him. A woman's voice answered him.

'Hello?' Then her voice was drowned by a horrible yowling.

'What the devil!' Jimmy exclaimed.

The woman went on: 'This is the Wapping Home for Stray Cats.'

'You're telling me!' And Jimmy slammed down the receiver.

He opened the callbox door.

'No go,' he said to the girl. 'Suppose your age *is* twenty? You haven't skipped a birthday or two?'

She shook her head. 'I know it was that number.'

'Wouldn't be 0202?' he persisted. 'There's a twenty in that.'

She pondered the possibility.

'Well — '

'We'll try it.'

This time a man's ripe Cockney voice answered. It was the sort of voice that sounded as if it was gurgling its way through a pint of beer. Instantly Jimmy recognized it, at the same time recalling that the number had struck a responsive chord somewhere at the back of his brain.

''Ullo? 'Starboard Light' 'ere — '

'More like it,' Jimmy chuckled. 'My old friend 'Lucky', eh?'

'Mister Strange?' 'Lucky' Mallory asked. 'Cripes, ain't seed yer for a month o' Sundays — '

'We'll remedy that in half an hour,' Jimmy said.

He rejoined the girl and told her he

thought he'd hit on something.

'You'd better come along with me,' he said as they returned to his car. 'If either of these men should happen to be at 'Lucky's' pub you'll be able to give me the tip. We can slip in through a side entrance into 'Lucky's' private room so there'll be no chance of you being spotted first.'

He headed the car in the direction of the Pool and London's waterfront.

Arriving at the 'Starboard Light', he left the girl in a little private room behind the saloon bar and then went in search of 'Lucky'. The outsize proprietor was on the customers' side of the bar, and extended a mammoth tattooed arm in greeting as Jimmy made his appearance.

'Ah, welcome, Mister — er — er — '
He broke off with a cough, suddenly remembering that it might be more discreet not to shout his name aloud — some people were inclined to be touchy when it came to announcing their identity in public. ' 'Ow are yer, guv'nor?' he asked instead.

Jimmy grinned at the other's display of discretion.

'Bearing up, 'Lucky', and glad to see you.'

'Same 'ere!' He came forward and asked in a lowered voice:

'Wot is it?'

'Scotch, thanks!' Jimmy deliberately misunderstood the other's portentous whisper.

'Okay,' 'Lucky' said, with an enormous wink. Then again the hoarse undertone. 'I meant wot's the trouble?'

Jimmy, still kidding him, answered:

'The usual — bad thirst!'

'Lucky' eyed him doubtfully for a moment. Then he leered and nodded. 'I get it!'

For the benefit of any of the customers who might be interested, he went on loudly; 'Well, guv'nor, I don't know nuffink about nuffink.' He coughed and added in Jimmy's ear: 'Come through to the back an' 'ave it on me.'

'A nice thought,' agreed Jimmy. He explained, as he followed the other, that the girl would be waiting in the private room, which information was greeted with leers, sly winks and nudges.

As they quitted the bar, someone called out from the swing doors: 'G'night, 'Lucky'!'

' 'Night, mate!' 'Lucky' responded genially, and then, observing the departing customer's companion, guffawed with heavy humour: 'Don't let yer pal there fall an' bust them milk bottles!'

The man guffawed in reply: 'If 'e do, I won't help 'im lap it up! Now, if it was beer, they might be worf busting!' And the two men went out, laughing loudly.

'Lucky' led the way into the little room where Helen Carlton awaited them. Jimmy introduced them, drinks were brought and then the fat man produced a box of cigars.

' 'Ere, Mister Strange, 'ave a ceegar?'

'Why, what have you got against me?'

'No, reely, these are a bit of orl right.'

'I'll bet they are.'

'Try one.' Volunteering heroically: 'I'll join yer.'

Dubiously Jimmy took a dark, evil-looking cigar, saying as the other followed his example:

'Well, if we're going to die *together*.'

They lit up, and after a moment Jimmy crossed to the window and gazed over the moonlit waterfront speculatively. He turned to 'Lucky' and queried casually: 'Anything been going on down here lately — unusual?'

'Unusual?'

'Come on, 'Lucky', do I have to drag it out of you?'

The other caught the sudden grim note in Jimmy's voice, and shot him a quick glance. He said slowly: 'Now you 'appens ter mention it, there 'ave been a coupler strangers hanging about.'

'Who would they be?'

'Lucky' scratched his head. 'I ain't properly caught on,' he muttered, 'yet.' Then added: 'One of 'em's called Saul Somebody-or-Other. Don't know the other bloke's name. Saul 'ad a 'phone call 'ere the other day. That's 'ow I know 'is name.'

Jimmy nodded and glanced inquiringly at the girl, quiet in the corner. She shook her head. The name meant nothing to her. They might be confederates of the kidnappers, however, Jimmy decided. He turned and asked:

'When was that 'phone call?'

'Day or two ago. Didn't 'ear wot was said. Not that I'd lissen — '

'Of course not, 'Lucky'.'

Jimmy held the cigar away from his nostrils and eyed it with repugnance. 'What do you know about this fellow Saul?' he asked, returning the cigar to his mouth with a wry face.

'Not much. He's got a little boat down the river 'ere. Just recent. That was 'im I spoke to 'as 'e and 'is mate was going out just now. 'Is pal'd bought a couple bottles o' milk orf me.'

'Milk?' Jimmy was suddenly alert.

' 'Sright. Dunno 'oo' 'is pal was — '

'You did say — *milk?*'

'Yus, white stuff wot they gives kids.'

'Exactly.' His eyes were narrow slits. 'Where's this boat?'

The girl had stood up as she realized the significance of his sudden interest in the other's reference to the purchase of the bottles of milk.

'Lucky' was saying:

'You can get a dekko of 'er from this winder.' He gestured with his cigar.

'That's 'er — to starboard — see 'er ridin'-light?' He squinted through the tobacco haze. 'Looks like someone's going aboard.'

Jimmy nodded. 'They're tying up a dinghy.'

'Saul and 'is pal, I reckon.' And added: ''Ope they enjoys their milk!' He shook his head with mock gravity. 'Don't trust blokes wot swill that stuff!'

'Maybe you've got something,' Jimmy commented, and drummed his fingers on the window-ledge thoughtfully. Without taking his gaze from the river, he said: 'You wouldn't happen to have your rowing boat handy?'

'I got it tied up out there, yus — but wot's bitin' yer?'

'The urge for some exercise. Like to come?'

'Okay,' 'Lucky' grunted. 'I'll sit an' watch yer.'

'I was afraid of that!'

He gave the girl a quick smile, and noted that she seemed much calmer and relaxed. She had even repaired her make-up, ravaged by tears and emotion. She answered his grin with a tremulous flicker across her freshly lipsticked mouth.

'Be all right here for a while?' he asked her. 'We shan't be long. I just want to take a look at that boat.'

'I'll be all right.'

He nodded, and 'Lucky' led the way out of the room, down a narrow passage and on to the waterfront. It was dark and cloudy, sharp squalls came up off the black river. Their cigars glowed like little live coals in the gloom.

'My boat's in 'ere,' 'Lucky' said, indicating a flight of stone steps ahead of them.

'Just a minute.' Jimmy paused suddenly and glanced back at the 'Starboard Light'. 'Wossup?' croaked 'Lucky' hoarsely.

'Merely a hunch about that girl.' He turned and retraced his steps, The other caught up with him, breathing stertor-ously.

'Wot abaht 'er?'

'We'll see,' Jimmy said, as they went back down the narrow passage. He threw open the door of the private room and stood on the threshold.

The room was empty.

'She's 'opped it! Bunked! Skedaddled!' 'Lucky' stared at him questioningly.

Jimmy took a slow pull at his cigar.

'As you succinctly put it,' he murmured, 'the lady has gone.'

He put in some fast thinking. It seemed to him there could be only two reasons why she'd disappeared. One, because she feared that as a result of his intervention in the search for the missing child she might, if she stayed with him, become involved with the police. The other angle was that she'd suddenly determined to take a hand in rescuing the kid off her own bat. Maybe she wanted to try and expiate the wrong she'd done.

'Wot yer going ter do abaht it?' the fat man at his side muttered.

He shrugged. 'Nothing I can do.' She must have followed them the moment they left her and gone her own way into the darkness.

There was no chance of finding her. 'Let's hope she won't fall into the river,' he said, 'or something.'

'Lucky' followed him out on to the waterfront again. In a few moments he was sitting comfortably in the stem of his little rowing boat, while Jimmy pulled rhythmically at the oars.

'Blimey! I ain't done this since Margate,' observed 'Lucky' luxuriously. 'Luvverly.'

'Glad you're enjoying it.'

'Ow's it going?'

'It'd go a helluva lot better if you'd get out and push!' Jimmy replied, not without bitterness. He was not used to strenuous exercise of this nature, and the other was no lightweight to pull along.

'Lucky's' rich chuckle broke off suddenly. He peered across the water. In a lowered tone he muttered: 'Someone's leavin' the boat. Its Saul and 'is pal in the dinghy. Duck down so's they won't see us.'

Jimmy stopped rowing and they kept out of sight. In a few minutes the sound of the other boat's oars died away.

'Wonder where they're off to?' Jimmy mused, and began thoughtfully to row on towards the boat the two men had just quitted. Quickly he drew alongside and silently tied up. No sound came from the vessel, and he stepped aboard.

'You'll 'ave to give me a 'and up,' 'Lucky' quietly called up to him. 'Me sea legs ain't wot they used to be!'

Moving cautiously, and followed by the heavily breathing 'Lucky', Jimmy moved across the deck to the small cabin. He ducked inside and snapped on his cigarette lighter to provide some illumination.

'Well, well!' he murmured, as he viewed the objects before him. 'Take a look at this, 'Lucky'.'

'Lucky' looked. His beery eyes widened in surprise then took on a paternal tenderness.

'Strewth!' he wheezed, 'Sleepin' peaceful as you like, too! Bless 'is little 'eart!''

★ ★ ★

Some fifteen minutes later. Inspector Crow, his jaw sunk in his coat, his beetling brows drawn together, struck a

Napoleonic attitude on the dockside. At his elbow Sergeant Warburton shivered as the squally gusts off the river caught his face. Behind them two police cars were drawn up, beside them police officers waited expectantly. Opposite, still moored as she had been when Jimmy stepped aboard her, lay Saul's boat.

'You say the woman said she *thought* the child might be hidden on the boat?' Crow growled from the side of his mouth.

'That's all, sir. She described the whereabouts of the vessel — near the 'Starboard Light' and so on — and then rang off.'

The Inspector grunted non-committally.

'All too ruddy mysterious for my liking,' he said. 'Women telephoning anonymously out of the blue. Probably someone trying to be funny, or some crackpot.'

'Except that this informant referred to the Halloran child,' Warburton reminded him in pedantic tones. 'So she must have been acquainted with some of the facts. In my opinion, she was the nurse-maid, of whom we still have no news, and may possibly have been attempting to trace the child and the kidnappers single-handed. Or, alternatively — '

'Will you shut your trap!' snapped the Inspector, turning on him irascibly. 'Or, alternatively, teach your grandmother to suck eggs!'

The other, wrinkling his nose delicately in mute disapproval of his superior's schoolboyish, ill-tempered interruption and standing first on one leg then on the other in embarrassment, fell silent.

Inspector Crow continued in his contemplation of the dark river.

Suddenly a dinghy, occupied by two men, appeared from behind a barge downstream. It headed for Saul's boat — and was in fact Saul himself and his companion returning. Almost simultaneously a spark of light appeared on the moored vessel. Then a flame spurted upwards, and clouds of smoke began to uncoil themselves.

'For Pete's sake!' exclaimed the Inspector. 'The boat's on fire!'

Lumbering into action, he snapped an order to Warburton: 'Get the fire patrol.'

As the Sergeant hurried off, Crow stumbled down a flight of dockside steps and floundered into a police launch which had been standing by for him. The launch immediately sprang into life, and cutting an ever-mounting spume of water before it, made for the burning boat. His eyes half closed against the flying spray, the Inspector observed that the dinghy bearing the two men had stopped and was now turning back in the direction whence it had come.

'If there is any child aboard,' he growled to a river policeman at his side, 'those swine have left it to burn.' With grimly anxious eyes he watched the nearing vessel, now a blazing hulk from stem to stem. Smoke blew into his face and the heat from the flames could already be felt. Then, as the launch manoeuvred to draw as near as possible to the boat, there came a sudden terrific explosion and spurts of fire shot across the water.

Crow ducked as bits of debris flew past him. When he looked round there was little to see — only a sizzle of smoke and steam from the river's surface and floating wreckage. For several minutes the police-launch cruised round the spot seeking vainly for any signs of life. There was nothing.

With a fervent prayer that the kidnapped child had not been aboard, Inspector Crow ordered the return of the launch to the dockside.

★   ★   ★

Back at Scotland Yard, the Inspector had little to show towards the recovery of the Halloran boy. In fact, he was preparing to face the strong possibility that the child must have been aboard the doomed vessel. Saul and his companion had been hauled in on the spot by the police, as a result of which the other two men actually responsible for carrying the child off in the car had been identified and their apprehension was merely a matter of a few hours. But Saul and the other man swore that they'd left the boy in the boat when they went ashore before the fire had started.

It was a disconsolate, defeated-looking Crow, therefore, who slumped over his office desk, his heavy-jawed features strangely bald where his beetling ginger eyebrows had been singed off by the flames from the explosion.

The telephone jangled, and he reached for it unenthusiastically. The next moment he was sitting bolt upright, and where his eyebrows should have been was raised in relief and surprise. It was Halloran, speaking excitedly in a nasal New York accent.

'Say, listen, Inspector! You don't have to worry any more about young Sammy — *he's home!*'

'What!'

'Yes, sir, safe and sound. Gosh, are we happy! I can't tell you — '

'But where — how — ?'

'Miss Carlton — his nurse — brought him back. She'd found out where the kidnappers had hidden him — '

'It was her who 'phoned us, then?'

'Maybe, maybe — I haven't asked her all the details. Too darned glad to see the kid. But there was a gentleman with her, and apparently they'd kinda cooperated — '

'Who is he?'

'Who is he? Well, I — er — pardon me, he's right here, as it happens.'

The Inspector heard some muffled words from Halloran's end, then a voice was chuckling in his ear — a voice that made him shoot up from his chair as if he'd sat on a tack.

'Hello, Crow, old bird — Strange, believe it or not, is the name.'

'*You*! How the hell — '

'I know, I *know*,' the voice purred over the wire. 'Disconcerting, isn't it, the way I bob up at the most unexpected moments? Just don't seem able to keep my nose out of your little troubles.'

'I don't want to talk to you, Strange,' the Inspector exploded. 'You're just a blasted — '

'Sshush!' Jimmy soothed him. 'Mustn't use naughty words, or Papa smack!'

Crow's face took on an apoplectic beetroot shade.

'Besides . . . ' that maddening voice went on, 'there's a lady present.'

'Get off the line!' roared Inspector Crow. 'I want to speak to Mr. Halloran — '

'Afraid you can't, Gorgeous. He's popped into the nursery to gurgle at his son and heir recently restored to his bosom — don't you wish *you'd* known a father's love?' Ignoring the other's bull-like bellowing, he went on smoothly, 'You can speak to Miss Carlton, the child's nurse, who's by my side. But no, on second thoughts, I'll speak to her myself. So long, you revolting old gargoyle.'

And Jimmy hung up.

He turned to the girl with a chuckle.

'And that would be roughly that.' After a moment, he went on thoughtfully; 'Good thing you were waiting for us when we came ashore with the kid. Not exactly my line of business, turning up here with it in my arms.' He grinned reminiscently. 'Though 'Lucky' looked even funnier — he's more used to bouncing roughs out of his bar than babes on his knee.'

'I came back as soon as I'd 'phoned Scotland Yard,' she said. 'I wasn't quite sure what I intended to do, I must admit, but — '

He regarded her for a moment. Then: 'Never mind, you showed willing and so long as your two — er — friends . . . ' She flinched and bit her lip. He went on: 'So long as they leave you out of it when they're pinched. And I somehow think they'll realize it wouldn't gain them extra sympathy, then I don't see why you shouldn't keep your job.'

'I've learned my lesson,' she said chokingly. 'And I'll never know how to thank you — '

'Glad to have been a help.'

As he turned to go, she asked:

'How did the boat catch fire?'

He grinned. ' 'Lucky's' fault. I gave him my cigar to finish for me, and I'm afraid he must've left it behind when we took the kid — very near a can of petrol. Careless of him, wasn't it?' His expression was enigmatic. 'Mind you, he didn't seem unduly depressed by the — er — accident. Don't think 'Lucky' cares very much for the baby-snatching type.'

It was only when getting into his car to

drive away he noticed the bottle of whisky and with a guilty start remembered Sandra. He gave a low whistle of shocked chagrin and stepped on the accelerator. His expression grew gloomier as he pictured her face on hearing his excuse for his late arrival. Looking for someone's lost baby.

Imagine Sandra believing that one!

And as he drew up outside her flat he realized with an ironically twisted smile that this was one time when he'd failed to think up a lie that would sound more convincing.

THE END

Books by Ernest Dudley
in the Linford Mystery Library:

ALIBI AND DR. MORELLE
THE HARASSED HERO
CONFESS TO DR. MORELLE
THE MIND OF DR. MORELLE
DR. MORELLE AND DESTINY
CALLERS FOR DR. MORELLE
LOOK OUT FOR LUCIFER!
MENACE FOR DR. MORELLE
NIGHTMARE FOR DR. MORELLE
THE WHISTLING SANDS
TO LOVE AND PERISH
DR. MORELLE TAKES A BOW
DR. MORELLE AND THE
DRUMMER GIRL
THE CROOKED STRAIGHT
MR. WALKER WANTS TO KNOW
TWO-FACE
DR. MORELLE AT MIDNIGHT
THE DARK BUREAU
THE CROOKED INN
THE BLIND BEAK
DR. MORELLE AND THE DOLL
LEATHERFACE

DR. MORELLE MEETS MURDER
A CASE FOR DR. MORELLE
DR. MORELLE'S CASEBOOK
DR. MORELLE INVESTIGATES
DR. MORELLE INTERVENES
SEND FOR DR. MORELLE
DR. MORELLE ELUCIDATES
DR. MORELLE MARCHES ON

We do hope that you have enjoyed reading this large print book.

Did you know that all of our titles are available for purchase?

We publish a wide range of high quality large print books including:
Romances, Mysteries, Classics
General Fiction
Non Fiction and Westerns

Special interest titles available in large print are:
The Little Oxford Dictionary
Music Book, Song Book
Hymn Book, Service Book

Also available from us courtesy of Oxford University Press:
Young Readers' Dictionary
(large print edition)
Young Readers' Thesaurus
(large print edition)

For further information or a free brochure, please contact us at:
Ulverscroft Large Print Books Ltd.,
The Green, Bradgate Road, Anstey,
Leicester, LE7 7FU, England.
Tel: (00 44) **0116 236 4325**
Fax: (00 44) **0116 234 0205**

*Other titles in the
Linford Mystery Library:*

THE MISSING HEIRESS MURDERS

John Glasby

Private eye Johnny Merak's latest client, top Mob man Enrico Manzelli, has received death-threats. A menacing man himself, he pressures Johnny to discover who was sending them — and why. Then Barbara Minton, a rich heiress, disappears, and her husband turns to Johnny. Despite Manzelli's ultimatum — that Johnny should focus on his case alone — he takes the job. But that's before he discovers the fate of the first detective Minton hired. And more bodies are stacking up . . .

A THING OF THE PAST

John Russell Fearn

Something was wrong, in and around London. Men were not shaving; women were becoming slipshod, dowdy and sullen-faced. People were bad-tempered, lacking self respect, and crime was on the increase. And, linked to these strange evidences of atavism, was a one-time excavation site. Now a mighty smoking crater, it looked as though a meteorite had descended . . . and from the vast fissure below the crater, there emerged the hideous survivors of a lost age of monster dinosaurs . . .

THE BLACK TERROR

John Russell Fearn

Troubled man Martin Clegg has always suffered from dreams which seem intensely real. In them, bizarrely, he's another person — not of this Earth! He's finally forced to confide in his fiancée, Elsie Barlow, and they consult Martin's scientifically inclined friend Tom Cavendish. He reveals, astonishingly, that Martin has a cosmic twin to whom he's mentally linked. Unsuspecting, they are about to become caught up in the strands of an incredible cosmic mystery that will, inexorably, be played out . . .

DR. MORELLE MARCHES ON

Ernest Dudley

Paula Webb visits Doctor Morelle with a startling confession. Believing that her former lover, nightclub owner Max Powers, had caused her sister's death, she shot him dead. A convincing story: Doctor Morelle and Miss Frayle were present outside the club when the police discovered Powers' dead body within. However, a suicide note is discovered — sufficient reason for the Doctor to suspect that Powers' death isn't what it seems — and to decide the case worthy of his legendary investigative talents . . .

OUIJA

Drew Launay

Warren Ryder had never believed in the supernatural. Until that fateful night when he jokingly asked the ouija to send him Jacinta — and the lovely young girl had come to his bedside. Now Jacinta was dead. He could still recall cutting down her blood-soaked body from the ceiling. For Warren, the ouija's game had just begun — a game of undying terror he could no longer control . . . Those who speak with the dead sometimes join them . . . in hell.

S.T.A.R. FLIGHT

E. C. Tubb

The Kaltich invaders are cruelly pro-
longing their Earthmen serfs' lives and
denying them the secret of instantaneous space travel, so desperately needed
by a barbaric, overpopulated Earth.
While the Kaltichs strip Earth of its
riches, the Secret Terran Armed Resistance movement, STAR, opposes them
— but it's only their agent, Martin
Preston, who can possibly steal the
aliens' secrets. If he fails, billions of
people will starve — with no place to
go to except to their graves.